MERRY MISRULE

ELLIE ST. CLAIR

♥ **Copyright 2020 Ellie St Clair**

All rights reserved.

This book or parts thereof may not be reproduced in any form, stored in any retrieval system, or transmitted in any form by any means—electronic, mechanical, photocopy, recording, or otherwise—without prior written permission of the publisher.

Facebook: Ellie St. Clair

Cover by AJF Designs

Do you love historical romance? Receive access to a free ebook, as well as exclusive content such as giveaways, contests, freebies and advance notice of pre-orders through my mailing list!

Sign up here!

Also By Ellie St. Clair

Christmas Books

A Match Made at Christmas
A Match Made in Winter

Christmastide with His Countess
Her Christmas Wish
Merry Misrule
Duke of Christmas
Duncan's Christmas

For a full list of all of Ellie's books, please see www.elliestclair.com/books.

CHAPTER 1

"You said he wouldn't be here."

"I did." Caroline cringed. "And I really didn't think he would be… but he surprised us all. Mother was astonished."

Joanna nodded, attempting to keep her expression neutral. She knew she should be happy for her friend and pleased for her entire family. Lord Elijah had been gone for over two years now, and they had all rejoiced at his early return from the war.

All but Joanna.

In fact, the only reason she was here was because she had been assured that Caroline's brother was still away.

For after the last time she had attended such a Christmas party at Briercrest, she had vowed to never be in his company again.

She eyed him suspiciously now from across the drawing room, where he sat in a giltwood Hepplewhite armchair, his eyes dark and heavy lidded, but she wasn't tricked by his nonchalant pose. He had a smoke in one hand, a drink in the other, a smug smile on his face. Typical, she thought with a snort, turning around to find her friend looking at her with both pity and apprehension.

"I know he wasn't the... nicest to you, Jo, and I have apologized more times than I can count. But he's really not a bad sort."

Caroline stared at her imploringly, as though she was hopeful that Joanna might change her mind.

She was not to be appeased.

Joanna raised her eyebrows. "Caro, because of him I refused to come visit your house for five years. Because of him I lost my most cherished possession left to me by my grandmother. Because of him, I came to dread Christmas."

"I know, Jo, I do," Caroline said, placing a hand on Joanna's arm as she cast her eyes downward. "I'll make him promise to behave himself."

"Because he always listens to you?" Joanna said wryly, knowing she wasn't being fair to her friend, but unable to stop herself.

"You make a point." Caroline sighed, running a hand over her hair, the same sinfully sweet chocolate as her brother's. "I promise to do my very best, however."

Joanna sighed, attempting a smile, but nearly failing, as she couldn't help but allow her gaze to wander across the expanse of crimson and gold Wilton carpet once more.

The worst of it all was that Lord Elijah Kentmore was just as handsome now, if not more so, than he ever was. Five years had aged him to near perfection. His skin had a touch of tan, passed down from an African grandmother, his hair dark with curls that had always made her wonder whether or not they would wrap perfectly around her finger. She wished she didn't know that his eyes were a beautiful shade of brown, with a navy circle around the outer edges.

But she did. She knew it all. And she hated him for how perfect his cheekbones were, how chiseled his jaw, how sensuous his lips that were always curled into that smile that beckoned, telling her that if she were to ever tempt herself with his sweetness, he would show pleasure of the highest order.

But that was exactly what had brought about her downfall years past. She was older now, more knowledgeable, and aware of just how he used his charms of seduction for mischief.

She would not be fooled again.

Just then, he turned, catching her eye, noticing her stare, and she jumped in shock, quickly snapping her gaze away to rest upon the flicker of the candlesticks over the fireplace before berating herself for her cowardice. Why should she be ashamed for staring? Everyone else was. She had good reason to.

She held her chin high as she turned her face back toward him proudly, as though she had nothing to hide.

And then he winked at her.

Joanna's chin dropped open in shock at the action for just a moment, but when he smiled smugly she promptly lifted it once more before turning away, now frantically searching for an escape. Seeing no conversation she had any wish to join, she decided instead that now would be a good time to give herself a tour of some of the front rooms of the house, to see what, if anything, had changed since her last visit to Briercrest Manor.

The skirts of her red silk drop-front gown, still one of her favorites and yet sadly a few years out of date, swished as she walked swiftly down the corridor, away from the drawing room that held tonight's musical entertainment.

The door of the library was cracked just a bit, and she pushed it open and stepped through, finding the room inviting with its warm fire blazing, the steady, solid bookshelves stacked from floor to ceiling, filled with the finest of tomes. She longed for a library like this, one which required a ladder to reach to the very highest shelf.

But at the moment, she was just lucky to be able to make it to the circulation library and borrow a single title.

The room was the same. Everything in the house was the same, it seemed, except her. She was the one who had changed. She sighed and turned to leave the room, but upon reaching the doorway, she came to an abrupt halt.

For there, blocking her exit, was the very man she was attempting to escape.

* * *

"Well, well, what — or should I say *who* — do we have here?"

Eli wasn't entirely sure who this woman was, but his sister had only a few close friends and was not prone to making new ones. He had seen Caroline conversing with her, and was instantly captivated by the woman, her striking features catching his eye from where he sat scanning the room from his corner.

He was attempting nonchalance, but the truth was, he felt much safer in the corner — where he could pretend to be the man he once was and not who he had become.

He had left England as Elijah Kentmore, charmer, schemer, practical joker.

The war had turned him into someone else entirely — someone, he was sure, this room of revelers were not yet ready to meet.

He found drinking a few cups of his father's fine port helped bring back his former self, removing the layers that had been added through his years at war.

He hadn't tried using women yet to do so, but he figured this one would do as good as any for experimentation.

She, however, did not seem entirely convinced.

"Did you follow me?" she asked, her green eyes turning stormy, but he enjoyed the fire emanating from them, even if it was an angry fire and not an amorous one.

"Would you like me to say yes?" he asked, flashing her a grin, but she was unmoved.

"I'd rather you didn't," she said, her mouth set into a grim line — a mouth of pretty pink lips that he would love to taste.

"Do you know where you're standing?" He quirked an eyebrow, a look that always worked with women — but it seemed this one was immune to his charms.

"In the doorway of the library," she said, unimpressed.

"And underneath the mistletoe."

"I am not," she said stonily, but then, after twitching a couple of times as she seemed to attempt to rein in control, she couldn't help herself. She looked up.

If her countenance could have grown grimmer, then it did.

She crossed her arms over her chest, squeezing the bodice of her gown — and her perfectly formed breasts — closer together.

Eli tried not to look. But he wasn't that good of a man.

His head dropped. So did her lips.

He had never seen a frown so somber, and he yearned to turn it upside down.

He leaned in closer to her. She leaned back. He stepped inside the door. She stepped back.

"It doesn't seem as if we are standing under the mistletoe any longer," she said. "And in fact, it could be argued that it was you who was doing so — not I. Now if you'll excuse me—"

"Who are you?" He couldn't help himself. He needed to know.

She stared up at him, her brows lifting and her eyes

widening before she peered closer at his face, pausing for a beat. "You're serious."

"How could such a question be asked in jest?"

Her lips parted in surprise. "You don't know who I am."

Why did she say it like a statement instead of a question? He searched her face. *Should* he know her? He supposed there was something familiar about her — but he couldn't quite place her.

"Err—"

"Unbelievable." She snorted, shaking her head.

"My apologies," he said, doing his best to show how contrite he really was, "but since this is a new acquaintance for one of us, perhaps we should start off on a right note."

He picked up her gloved hand, raising it, pressing his lips to it before she wrenched it away.

"Lord Elijah Kentmore."

"I don't think—"

He swiftly stepped toward her, wrapping an arm around her back and dipping his head to kiss her before she could protest any further — they were below the mistletoe, after all — but before his lips touched hers, she ducked underneath his arm and was on the opposite side of him.

"What do you think you are doing?" she asked, two splotches of red appearing on her cheeks. He wished they were from desire, but he came to the unfortunate conclusion that they were most likely caused by anger. He scratched his head.

"Well, we were underneath the mistletoe, and—"

She lifted a hand, and he flinched, for a moment anticipating a slap, but instead she held her finger in the air in admonishment.

"If you ever— and I mean ever— attempt to kiss me again, especially without my permission, then you will regret ever coming home. Do you understand me?"

She was rigid, practically shaking with fury, and Eli finally realized that whatever notion this woman held toward him, it was of the very worst sort.

"I understand," he said softly, taking a step back, also realizing just how grossly he had misconstrued the situation. "And I am sorry — for this, and for whatever wrong I have caused you to suffer."

For a moment, her anger dropped, but she seemed to steel it back up again.

"If only it were so simple," she said, shaking her head. "But the fact that you don't even remember *me*, let alone what happened — well, that says more than any apology ever could."

He could do naught but watch helplessly as she stormed away down the hallway, her red skirts furiously snapping around her legs.

"Joanna?" A voice called out.

He whipped his head around as he saw his sister emerging from the drawing room, following the unknown woman down the hall.

"Jo—Eli?" She stopped when she saw him, looking back and forth between the woman's retreating back and where he stood with his hands on his hips.

"Oh, Eli," she tilted her head as she looked at him with dismay, "what did you do?"

"What do you mean, what did I do?" he said defensively. Why did everyone always think he had done something?

Probably because he usually had. He rubbed his brow, dismayed that nothing had changed here — especially his family's regard toward him.

"Did you talk to Joanna?"

"Joanna?"

"Yes," she said, pointing to the red dress that was now rounding the corner away from them. "Did you talk to her?"

"Perhaps," he muttered. "But tell me — just who *is* Joanna?"

Now it was his sister's mouth that fell open.

"You don't remember Joanna?" she asked. "My closest friend, Joanna Merryton? The one who used to spend Christmas with us when we were home from finishing school? The one you tortured?"

"Tortured? I don't recall ever torturing anyone. I know I played a few practical jokes, sure, but—"

Suddenly he realized just who she was talking about.

"Joanna? *That* woman is Joanna?"

It was his turn to be shocked.

"That can't be the same Joanna. Your friend Joanna is... well, she was... plain. Pudgy. Pedestrian. This woman is stunning."

From what he could remember, anyway.

"Yes." Caroline crossed her arms over her chest. "She is. She is one of those women who took some time to grow into her looks."

Had she ever. Her pudginess had developed into delicious curves. Her hair, which at the time had always been pulled back into tight braids around her head, now was shiny, sleek, polished. Her green eyes would have previously been hidden by spectacles. Those, it seemed, were now gone as well.

She had been awkward. Now she was astonishing.

He realized he was still staring down the hallway.

"Did I... did I do anything to her to cause her such disregard for me?"

"Do you truly have no memory of her at all?" Caroline asked, one eyebrow crooked.

She was partially right. He was lacking a few memories, but now wasn't the time to share all of his failings with his sister.

"Er... they are somewhat foggy. Can you enlighten me?" he asked.

"Well, there was the time you pretended you were going to kiss her underneath the mistletoe and then held out the dog instead while all of your friends watched."

Eli swallowed hard.

That could explain her hesitancy when he had pointed out where they had found themselves.

"And then there was the time that you placed coal in her stocking, replacing all of the gifts Mother had bought for her — gifts that would have been the first she had received in years."

"No..."

"But worst of all, was the time when you stole the pocket watch her grandmother had given her, then gave it to Cecily Cummings for Christmas because you were sweet on her. Joanna went to Cecily and begged for its return, but Cecily refused."

Eli's own cheeks were warming now.

"I really did all that? Are you sure you're not just embellishing? I mean—"

"You did," she said, her eyes narrowing, "and I had to continue to apologize for it. I'm not saying that you did it alone but it was you who perpetrated it. So if you are wondering just why she wasn't pleased to see you, now you know. The truth is, Elijah, she doesn't even want to be in the same house as you, and the only reason she agreed to come was because she thought you were still at war. So please, *please*, just leave her alone. Do you understand?"

He nodded.

But he didn't agree. For he had a new Christmas wish.

To win over Joanna Merryton.

CHAPTER 2

Joanna paced her bedchamber, inwardly fuming but unable to do anything about it. After all, this was Lord Elijah's home — not hers.

She could be as angry as she wanted to be, as hurt as she wanted to be, but at the end of it all, it didn't really matter. She had chosen to come here, and, for these two weeks, was living off of the generosity of the Kentmore family.

Besides, her own protestations were silly. So she had lost a pocket watch years ago — even though it had been one of the few tokens she had left to remember the woman who had raised her, it was still just a token. Elijah had risked his life at war. She should be happy he was home.

In fact, she had always found it rather difficult over the past few years to reconcile the boy she had known with a man who would put himself in danger for his country. Perhaps he hadn't had any idea what he was getting himself into. Perhaps he only did it for the reputation and the valor that came along with it. She couldn't see any other reason.

She stopped when she caught a glimpse of herself in the mirror on the small, simple vanity, and she walked over, placing her hands on the glossy wood surface before her. Squinting slightly to properly see, she ran her eyes over the heightened color in her cheeks, her hair standing on end, her dress bunched where the ties had come loose.

And she was reminded of another woman — one not much more than a girl, really. One had nothing but a job as a seamstress, the smallest of shared spaces in London to call home, a few women she was lucky enough to call her good friends, and the memory of a grandmother who had loved her. She used to live for the days she could come visit with her closest friend, Caroline — until her friend's brother had ruined everything for her.

For the worst of it was that Eli had always been so bright, so handsome, so stunning, that there wasn't a woman who met him that didn't want him for herself. And for just a moment, five years ago, Joanna had been amazed that he had chosen her — pudgy, plain her — even if it was for just one kiss beneath the mistletoe.

And then he'd lifted the pug to her face instead.

The memory of it — and of the laughter that had echoed around her when she had sprung back in horror — was as clear in her mind as tonight's encounter.

She couldn't stay. Not with him here.

Thank goodness Caroline and Lord Alexander had been there to comfort her. Lord Elijah had tried to blame his brother for all of it, but that had all been a lie. Just like Lord Elijah's trickery.

Joanna pushed away from the plain mahogany vanity, rounding the corner of the tall bed, its soft white canopies brushing against her face, either taunting her or tempering her, she wasn't entirely sure which. She crossed over to the wardrobe, pulling it open to be greeted by the forlorn few dresses that seemed to long for company in the barren space.

At the bottom, she found what she was looking for — her

worn, frayed valise. She tossed it on the bed, opening it up before she returned to the wardrobe and began to pull down the few dresses that had accompanied her. She had done her very best to mend them to a desirable state, and had altered the dresses that Caroline had insisted upon giving her. Joanna could but hope that no one would recognize them and realize that she had become such a charity.

And then there was the final dress. Joanna pulled it out reverently. She was only in possession of it because the woman who had commissioned it decided she no longer wanted it. Joanna had spent hours on it, and while she was out a considerable amount of time, when Caroline had invited her to the house party over Christmas, Joanna had decided to allow herself this small luxury and had asked for permission to borrow it.

The owner of her small shop had allowed it, for a deduction of her pay, but Joanna had thought it would be worth it, for at least she would look something like the other women this Christmas.

She had been wrong.

She would spend Christmas in London, alone once again.

Joanna was startled when a knock sounded on the door, and she crossed over to it, expecting Caroline.

She found someone else entirely.

"Lord Elijah," she said, not so much in greeting but in surprise. "What are you doing here?"

"I live here."

She closed her eyes for a moment, not prepared for his teasing — even if, this time, it was meant in humor.

"What are you doing in my bedchamber?"

She opened her eyes as she spoke, but instantly regretted doing so. For then his chocolate eyes were boring into hers, warming her from deep inside.

She hated that he could so affect her with just one look.

"I am here to apologize," he said, slightly bowing toward her, and her eyes widened.

"For…?"

"For many things," he said, sweeping an arm out in front of him, and she couldn't help but notice how fine he looked in his red jacket, grey waistcoat, and buff breeches, displaying with much definition just how much he had grown into a man over his years away. "For attempting to kiss you when you had no desire for my touch. For everything I did to you years ago, which Caroline describes as horrible, horrible acts. And for forgetting you."

He lifted a hand as though he was going to brush it against her face, but when she flinched slightly, he let it fall back to his side.

"Forgive me — again. I'm afraid I am not used to many women rejecting my interest and it has been some time since I have been within society."

Joanna lifted an eyebrow. It was quite the admission, and yet, a few words could not erase all that he had done in the past. Anyone could apologize. But his very actions tonight had proven that he hadn't much changed since she had known him years ago.

"I was one of those women once, who fell for your charms," she said, pulling herself up to her full height, which was still a good head shorter than he. "But that proved to be a mistake and I have since learned my lesson when it comes to you."

"So Caroline shared with me," he said, dipping his head. "I was an immature lad who thought I was making some great joke."

"At my expense."

"Yes, at your expense," he admitted with a nod. "I have come to offer you my regrets and to invite you back to the party. I did not mean to scare you away."

"I can look after myself just fine," she said smartly. "Your actions do not affect me." A lie, but a necessary one.

He seemed relieved. "Glad to hear it. I— what are you doing?"

"Freshening up." Another lie.

"No." He pushed past her and stepped farther into the room. "Your bag is out. As are your clothes. Are you going somewhere?"

"No."

Yes.

"And would you please get out of my room?" she continued. "This isn't at all seemly."

He waved a hand. "No one particularly cares. They're all downstairs making merry."

He turned around suddenly, his commanding presence so close to the bed overwhelming her. She wished he would just leave.

"Please go," she said, as though her intentions had not been clear before, but he leaned forward and scrutinized her more closely.

"You *are* leaving."

"I…" releasing a frustrated sigh, she gave up arguing, "yes. I am leaving. I have decided to return to London in the morning."

"I should hope not on my account."

Yes, on his account. And if she hadn't wanted to leave before, as she'd been packing, she had glimpsed through her window Cecily Cummings, or whatever her name was now, alighting from a carriage and entering the manor. Now Briercrest held both of the people she most never wanted to see again.

While she said nothing, he must have gathered her thoughts from the expression on her face.

"Please," he said, and Joanna's eyes widened when she

realized that he was practically begging her. "Please don't go. Caroline would have my hide. She was quite looking forward to your visit. I promise you that I shall be on my best behavior. We shall pretend nothing ever happened in the past, and I shall stay as far from you as you choose. Is that fair?"

Joanna sighed. She had been looking forward to spending time with Caroline as well. Her friend had remained here in the country since the summer, and as Joanna now lived in London, she had little opportunity to see her. If Eli was willing to keep his distance…

"Very well," she finally gave in, "but I will decide so for Caroline, not for you."

"Splendid," he said, beaming, "she shall be extraordinarily pleased."

His face softened for a moment, and she wondered whether he was actually showing some vulnerability or if this was all an act.

"I am sorry, Miss Merryton, truly I am. I'm not used to polite company, having spent so long away, and even before then—"

"You were not much one for the entire politeness aspect?" she said wryly, and he chuckled.

"I suppose not."

Joanna nearly laughed herself, but then she remembered who he was and that he always knew exactly what to do and say to keep himself from trouble — trouble which she had no time or energy for. She had been provided a brief respite from her work, but after this time away, it would be back to hours bent over her needlework once more, for this was the one holiday she would receive this year. This time had been hard worked for and should not be taken for granted.

"I am sorry."

"You have said that a few times," she said, finished with it all and no longer caring if anything she said to him was offensive in the least. "But are you truly sorry about what you said, or are you merely sorry because now I have become a woman you wouldn't mind kissing under the mistletoe?"

And with her nose in the air, she brushed by him and out into the corridor, quite proud of herself and her retort.

She knew it wasn't entirely true. She would never be as beautiful a woman as Cecily — Lady Danvers now — or Caroline, but, from the change in attention from young men she encountered, she was aware that she no longer blended into the wallpaper and the furniture as she once did.

She only hoped she had made him think, so that the next poor soul he tried to capture under the Christmas canoodling bough wouldn't go through what she did.

For one thing was certain — no matter how handsome, how charming, how apologetic he was, that woman most certainly would never again be her.

CHAPTER 3

*E*lijah was captivated.

He'd like to say it was because no other woman had ever spurned him so. No other woman had been uninterested in his advances. No other woman had ever spoken to him with such forthrightness, so unapologetic in her words toward him.

But it was more than that.

There was something about Miss Joanna Merryton. She was beautiful, in a fresh, unique way. Her green eyes reminded him of emeralds, but they were a bit too shrewd and just a bit too far apart from one another. They also had a bit of a cross-eyed look when she squinted that made him wonder whether her lack of spectacles was a choice.

Her hair was a mix between gold and chestnut, sleek and fine, but also seemingly as straight as could be from what he could tell. The ringlet that seemed to be attempting to surround her face when he'd first sought her out had been nearly straight by the time he had left her room. Her cheekbones were high, and a dimple emerged every now and then when her mouth curled into a smile, even if it was a wry one — as it seemed to be whenever she looked at him.

Maybe it was the way she held her nose in the air when she glanced his way, as though she was trying to convince herself that she was better than he and his rash behavior. He wasn't sure, but, try as he might, he couldn't stop looking at her throughout the entire dinner that evening.

And this was but the first day of the Christmas party to be held at Briercrest.

A Christmas party he had never expected.

While he had been on the front lines, suffering from rations and lack of cheer, somehow he had assumed that everyone at home would be of an equally low morale.

He had been entirely wrong. His family seemed in as good of spirits as ever. He had been as astonished as they when he had knocked on the door, only to find them preparing for a house full of guests.

As a matter of fact, they had to rearrange his bedroom for him once more, as the maids had been in the process of preparing it for one of the couples who were to join them.

They had assumed that he would be overjoyed by the party — for Elijah had always been known to love company. Little did they know that he had been looking forward to some peace and quiet.

That, however, did not seem to be part of his near future. At least, not until after Christmas. A Christmas that would hopefully pass quickly.

When he returned to the party, it was nearly time for dinner, and he wanted nothing more than to approach Miss Merryton to lead her in and to reacquaint himself with her. He cursed his memory, which, no matter how hard he wished it, was never going to be the same again. It had been annoying, but up to this point, he hadn't much cared. Now, though, he had something to care about, for it seemed he had lost full memories of Joanna Merryton. Memories which, according to his sister and Miss Merryton, were not particularly good ones to begin with.

He retook his seat across the drawing room, his eyes half shuttered as he watched her speak with Caroline, who was likely apologizing for his behavior yet again. He was so intent in his study that he nearly didn't notice Cecily and her husband approach.

"Elijah! How wonderful to see you! We are such old friends we can dispense with formalities, can we not?" she gushed. Cecily always gushed, as though every time she spoke to someone it was the height of excitement. He supposed it wasn't the worst trait a person could possess, but it did become rather annoying after a time — especially when he knew that she was just as likely to turn around and gossip about everything she had just learned after one of her conversations. "I'm not sure if you have even met Robert before, have you? Or, should I say, Lord Danvers?"

"Ah—" Elijah couldn't entirely remember as he stood to greet them, but fortunately Danvers solved the problem for him.

"Of course, Kentmore and I go back to our school days at Eton. How are you, old chap? Heard you had gone off to war. Wasn't sure if we'd be seeing you here, after hearing the tales of your injury. That was a bad bit of luck. Good to see you're in fine health."

Eli was somewhat taken aback that the story of his misfortune had already circulated through England. But, then, news of other's misery seemed to travel faster than anything more pleasant.

"All is fine," Elijah said with what he hoped was an easy smile. "A small injury, and I was ready to come home as it was."

"Oh, yes!" Cecily exclaimed, bringing her hands together

in front of her as she looked at him with a benevolent smile. "I could hardly believe it when I heard you had been hurt. You always seemed to be... untouchable."

Elijah pressed his lips tightly together, hoping his expression wasn't a grimace. As he looked around to see if dinner was going to be served anytime soon, he noticed that Joanna had drifted closer toward him, and he wondered if she could hear their conversation — and if she would even care about it if she did.

She was speaking to Admiral Cuthbert at the moment, however, and he knew from experience that it was difficult to hear anything else when the admiral was in close proximity. He was a man Elijah could never forget, as the admiral had been such a close friend of his father for many years now.

He could practically hear the admiral bellowing in Miss Merryton's ear, but then, the admiral bellowed so much that one became used to the sound. Eli was just preparing to rise and save her — although he doubted she would see it as such — when his younger brother, Alexander, appeared beside her, offering his arm, no doubt to lead her in to supper.

Elijah fell back into his chair, feeling sorry for himself, even though any cause for discord between him and Miss Merryton was entirely of his own doing.

If only he were more like Alex. Alex, who always seemed to do the right thing, even when he was participating in Elijah's schemes, or encouraging him into it.

It would even be an improvement to be like Baxter, he supposed, looking across the room at his eldest brother, who was currently entertaining a circle of guests before leading them into the dining room. Baxter was just like their father — a touch obnoxious and prone to drink, but also a responsible, careful host, the perfect lord in every way.

Thank goodness Baxter — Lord Baxter — already had

two sons, now that the new baby had arrived, meaning the line would never fall into Elijah's own unfortunate hands. As Cecily and her husband wandered off, Elijah supposed that he'd best take himself in to supper, for it seemed that no one would be waiting for him. Which was how it usually was.

Elijah, the forgotten one.

And how it should probably remain.

* * *

JOANNA ATTEMPTED to maintain a look of interest on her face as Lord Alexander and the admiral began speaking of his days at sea, although she wasn't above taking the opportunity to begin slinking back and away from the conversation.

She appreciated Lord Alexander's approach, allowing her an escape, and she noted how courteous he was — always there to lend a hand when needed. So unlike Lord Elijah.

Lord Elijah was sin. Temptation. Everything she normally ran from.

But she couldn't seem to avoid him.

That was the truth of it, the real reason she wanted to leave — because she didn't know if she would be able to hold herself back from him. She had seen him at his very worst, and yet still, she couldn't help herself from desiring more time with him, even if it would only lead to ruin — her own ruin.

Fortunately, they were soon called for dinner, and Lord Alexander led her to a place far down at the end of the table — surely far enough away that she wouldn't be tempted to engage in any conversation with Lord Elijah. She hadn't been able to help herself from eavesdropping on his conversation earlier with Cecily — Lady Danvers — and her husband. She still found it rather difficult to look at Cecily without malice, knowing that she still held onto her grandmother's gift.

Why she wouldn't give it back to her all of those years ago, Joanna didn't know, but she was always on the lookout for it to appear, wondering if maybe — just maybe — she might be able to filch it back.

Which wasn't really stealing, was it, if it was your own to begin with?

Fortunately, Caroline sat down on her right, giving her hand a quick squeeze as she did so.

"Thank you for staying," she said softly. "I know having Elijah here changes things, but he has honestly been on his best behavior since he arrived. He has promised to stay far from you, and I promise that since he has returned, he hasn't shown much sign of mischief. I think it might be possible that Eli has finally grown up."

Joanna didn't want to share her encounter with Lord Elijah with his sister — somehow it seemed wrong, even if it would prove to Caroline that he wasn't quite as mature as she thought.

"That would be lovely," was all she said instead but then noticed that Caroline wasn't paying her the slightest bit of attention any longer.

"Caro?" she asked, leaning forward to try to see into Caroline's face as the first course emerged from the kitchen. "Are you that hungry?" she asked, attempting laughter, but Caroline's attention was solely focused on the tureens of soup being carried in — one brown, one white, which would go alongside the remainder of the dishes, some already placed on the table and others carried in by various footmen.

Except... it seemed that Caroline only cared about the soup. Was it the soup she was staring at, however, or... did her gaze travel beyond?

Joanna studied the footman more closely. He was quite attractive, but then, most footmen were, particularly in a household like that of the Marquess of Darlington. The footman's blond hair waved at the top, and his blue eyes were fixed upon Caroline with an intensity that nearly took Joanna aback.

"Caro," she said in a stage whisper, poking her friend in the side, for suddenly she noticed that she was not the only one who seemed interested in the connection between the two of them.

Lord Elijah had taken up a seat across the table and three chairs down from her, right beside Lord and Lady Oxford, a pleasant couple who seemed to be quite infatuated with one another, causing Joanna to sigh with envy she wished away.

Lord Elijah had been in mid-conversation with them, but now he was looking back and forth between his sister and the footman — the footman who had come to a halt right beside Caroline, and was now placing the bowl of soup in front of her with the utmost care.

"My lady," he practically breathed, and Joanna wondered if everyone else could feel the air grow tense between them. She hoped that the scent of the greenery that lined the tables as well as the beeswax of the candles that were strewn through the room hid it all.

Maybe she just knew her friend better than most. Maybe no one else would notice anything was amiss.

"You there," Lord Elijah called from across the table, and the footman looked around as though searching, until he seemed to realize he was the one being addressed. "Yes, you. What's your name?"

"Thatcher, my lord."

"Thatcher. Do you see something you like here?" He grinned, but the look in his eyes was one of knowing, one of suspicion, one she didn't overly like.

Thatcher jolted upright at being addressed, as all of the eyes around the table suddenly turned toward him. As he did so, his tray tilted forward, the remaining bowl of soup upon it crashing to the tabletop, the floor, and spilling all over Caroline and Joanna, although Caroline suffered the worst of it.

"Oh!" she shouted, jumping from her chair as the brown soup now covered her cream silk gown. "It's hot!"

"Here," Joanna leaped up next to her, lifting their pieces of linen from the table and wiping the soup off Caroline's skin.

"We'll clean you up. Excuse us," she said, curtsying to the table, before conveying Caroline out of the room as quickly as she was able, as Caroline's father began to make apologies to the rest of the guests.

Joanna paused in the doorway, looking back just long enough to allow her gaze to rest on Lord Elijah. She narrowed her eyes at him, as he was already sitting back smugly, one arm resting upon the table as he sipped his drink and his soup.

Mature, indeed.

CHAPTER 4

"Out with it."

Caroline whirled around, her skin clear of soup, clad in a clean gown. Joanna would have changed herself, but she had nothing else to wear — not if she was planning to remain here for the rest of the house party. A few soup stains, half blotted out with a piece of linen, would have to stay.

"What do you mean?" Caroline asked, widening her eyes as she attempted innocence, but Joanna was already shaking her head at her.

"Your lady's maid is gone now, so you can tell me all. Has anything actually happened between you and the footman, or is this merely the two of you desiring what can never be?"

"It is... oh Joanna—" Caroline moaned, sitting down upon the bed next to her, taking her hands within hers as she bent over them in supplication. "I love him."

"You do?" Joanna asked, slightly shocked at Caroline's admission. To have a flirtation was one thing, but to be in love... "How did this happen?"

"I don't even properly know," Caroline said, throwing

herself backward on the bed. "I was here all summer, and then when my mother and father went to London for a month in September, I remained with my brother and his wife, as she was due to have her third baby and I felt like I should stay with her. She mostly remained in bed, however, and my brother was busy, so I was on my own. Samuel and I just got to talking one day and... well, we got on rather well. I know it is shocking—"

Joanna gave a low chuckle. "Not really. I am the granddaughter of a seamstress — a seamstress myself now — and you and I have always been the best of friends. I'm sure Thatcher's family is not that different from mine."

"I suppose," Caroline said, sitting up once more, leaning back on her elbows now.

"No one else knows?" Joanna asked, surprised how it could remain a secret if Caroline and Thatcher had been regarding one another with such open longing for any length of time.

"No," Caroline said remorsefully. "No one. Except now you, and obviously Elijah noticed."

"He most certainly did," Joanna said wryly. "And now because of him, Thatcher might lose his position."

"Do you think he would, truly?" Caroline asked, looking up at Joanna with concern. "For that little incident?"

"Caroline!" Joanna said, trying not to laugh at how lovesick her friend was to look past such a thing. "This is your world far more than it is mine. Think how you would feel if anyone else had poured a bowl of soup all over you. What would you expect?"

"You're right," she said morosely, the corners of her perfectly shaped lips drooping uncharacteristically, for Caroline was a woman who loved to laugh. "I shall have to have a talk with my father. As for Eli—"

Joanna looked over at her friend with one raised eyebrow. "I have an idea."

"You do?"

"I do," she said, her lips beginning to curl at the thought. "Lord Elijah loves a practical joke, does he not? Well, then, let's show him one."

* * *

ELIJAH HAD ALWAYS BEEN of the opinion that one of his redeeming qualities was the ability to admit when he was wrong.

And he had been wrong to call out the noticeable attention between his sister and the footman.

But he had spoken before he even realized what he was doing. He had seen the man staring at her so openly, so admiringly, which hadn't particularly bothered him — until he saw Caroline's return expression. Then he hadn't been able to keep his mouth shut.

He knew his sister wouldn't be pleased, but at the very least, he talked his father into reconsidering the man's firing until after Christmas. It hadn't made up for his mistake, but it was something.

"You don't really think that Caroline is carrying on with a *footman*," his father said in response to Elijah's request, a sentiment to which his mother only laughed at as the three of them were seated in his father's study following dinner. They didn't have much time — they would have to return to the party soon — but Elijah had asked for a moment alone.

"Of course she would never," his mother said, waving heavily ringed fingers in the air. "Caroline knows her place. She does spend far too much time with the Merryton girl, but at least she has some noble blood running through her veins."

"She does?" Elijah asked, much more interested in the conversation now that it had shifted.

"Yes, dear," his mother said, folding her hands in her lap. "Her father was the second son of Viscount Edgewater."

"What happened to him?" Elijah asked, wondering if he had ever asked about the story before, or whether it was one of his fleeting memories.

"You don't know?" his mother eyed him with her sharp, blue-eyed gaze, and he shook his head slowly.

"No, I don't think so."

"After his wife — Miss Merryton's mother, a woman far below him who he never should have married in the first place — left him for a pirate of all things, he basically ignored the girl. Her grandmother finally took her in. Her father still paid for her education and such, but when Miss Merryton was seventeen, he died penniless. His elder brother passed soon afterward and the title passed on to a cousin of some sort. Joanna learned the work of her grandmother."

His mother said the words with a shudder as though even mentioning it was going to cause her to catch some kind of affliction.

His father rolled his eyes. His own mother had spent her life working until she had met his father and become a marchioness. While he had known a life of relative luxury, he was not impervious to the lives of those a class below him.

"What seems to be the problem?"

Baxter walked in now, Lady Baxter — Ophelia — behind him. If Elijah hadn't known better, he would have thought they were a copy of his parents, but twenty years younger.

"It's taken care of," he said abruptly, not wanting Baxter involved, but of course, his brother couldn't help himself. He never had been able to.

"Is it about the footman business?" he said with a snort. "I hope you told him to pack his bags."

"Although his spill *was* partially Elijah's fault," Ophelia said, wrinkling her long, thin nose. "Are you going to have him pack his bags too?"

Elijah sat back and crossed his arms over his chest. He knew his sister-in-law was trying to make a joke, but he couldn't say he was overly pleased by it.

Even though she was right.

"The footman can stay for now," his father said with a sigh, as though he would prefer this entire business had not been brought before him. "I suppose it is Christmas, after all."

"Yes, it is."

Elijah didn't even turn to look at the door. His father's study was large, yes, but there was hardly enough seating for the lot of them. Caroline didn't appear to require a chair, however, as she remained rooted in her place near the door.

Elijah finally turned to look at her, more out of curiosity to see if she had changed her dress. She had. And she was accompanied by their brother, Alexander, who took in the scene with an expression of interest on his face, so very like Elijah's own reflection.

"What is the matter with you, Eli?" Caroline asked, staring at him hotly with her arms folded over her chest. "That was *not* well done of you."

"I think we should talk about this later," he murmured, not wanting to bring any further ire upon her. If she truly was carrying on with the footman, he would prefer to handle it his own way, without his brother and his father interfering, for he knew they would only make things worse, forcing Caroline right into the footman's arms.

"You were rude," she said, holding her chin high, "and I think you should apologize."

"To the footman?" he asked, raising his brows. "I can hardly see why. While I should not have said anything, it is still his job to place the soup on the table and not on your lap."

"Elijah, you, out of anyone, should know to be nicer."

"I should, should I?"

"Yes. You must have served with all kinds of men!" she exclaimed, throwing her hands in the air. "Did everyone not bleed the same?"

"I… I suppose so," he said with a shrug, although much of his time in the war was kind of hazy, if he was being honest. She had a point, though. Although, as officers, the gentlemen were less likely to be killed.

"There isn't actually anything happening between you and the footman, is there, darling?" their mother asked, her words nonchalant, although if Elijah knew her as well as he thought he did, he suspected there was an underlying hint of reproach and question there.

"No, of course not," Caroline said, although her eyes flashed for a moment with a knowing that Elijah wondered about, but she looked off at the secretaire in the corner too quickly for him to make anything of it.

"What do you think of Lord Cristobel?" Baxter asked, leaning toward his sister, and Elijah wondered if she didn't shudder slightly.

"Why does it matter?"

"He is interested in you."

"He is not!" Caroline exclaimed, as though she hadn't thought much on the fact that the single viscount had been invited to their Christmas party.

"He is." Baxter nodded, grinning now. "And he would like to be the recipient of your affections by the end of Christmastide."

"You're joking," Caroline said, her hands on her hips now, as Alexander's eyes followed the conversation with interest.

"I'm not," Baxter said with a smug smile. "We said we would help him, did we not, Ophelia dear?"

"We did," she confirmed with a nod of her head. "It would be quite the match."

"It would," his father chimed in. "I asked Baxter to find a potential match for you Caroline, and he thought Lord Cristobel would be a fine choice. I agree."

"I never asked for you to do so!"

"No, you didn't. But it's time."

"I never should have come in here," Caroline said with a toss of her head. "Family meetings — at least in *this* family — are always a mistake."

And with that, she was out the door, pulling it smartly shut behind her.

Elijah sighed as he rose and followed her. What a Christmas homecoming this was turning out to be.

CHAPTER 5

"*Is* this how you imagined your Christmas visit here with us?" Caroline asked Joanna wryly the next day as they stepped out the front door of the manor, drawing their cloaks tightly around themselves as the wind did its best to toss them away. Fortunately it had brought warm air today, and Joanna wouldn't have to worry about the cold that always seemed to invade beneath her skin.

"No," Joanna admitted with a sigh, "but then, the last time I was here, we were girls. We thought that one look from a young man meant he was in love."

They laughed at that as they skipped down the steps to meet the rest of the party. They were going for a walk through the family's grounds, although there wasn't much to see now that most of the greenery had browned and a layer of snow covered everything. There was, however, a small lake nearby and a few of the party brought skates.

Joanna and Caroline had a few games of their own in mind.

Briercrest had beautiful pasture in the summer — miles

of greenery stretching toward the tenants' homes dotting the hill as far as one could see.

Joanna had only seen the grounds covered in white once before — every other Christmas had been brown. And while she was aware of the difficulties snow could bring in terms of travel and the work required of the staff, she had to admit that she loved the beauty of the frost lining the tree branches, the chill seeming like diamonds in the air.

Their party had grown since the previous evening, and they made quite the drawn-out group as they plodded along.

Joanna's hip was bumped and she nearly took Caroline down with her, but she smiled when she saw the eagerness on the faces of the children as they raced by her. Christmas could be a time of such joy, she remembered, although it had been some years since it had been so for her. Since her grandmother had been alive.

"There it is!" Caroline cried excitedly. "The lake."

She craned her neck around — looking for Thatcher no doubt, but he was nowhere to be found, and she had to settle for Joanna's company instead.

It was a small yet pretty lake surrounded by evergreens and frosty trees. In previous years, the ice hadn't been thick enough to skate on it, but this year had proven to be just cold enough for them to enjoy it.

Some of their party sat down on a blanket laid out by the few footmen who had accompanied them and began to lace their skates, while many of the children simply slid out on the ice with their boots.

This was what Christmas was about, Joanna thought, putting all concerns about Elijah to the side. It was about family and fun and a time to find joy. Even if that joy was fleeting.

Caroline, as it happened, had not forgotten their plan of revenge.

"Over there," she said, pointing to a thatch of evergreens. "Little Clementine has agreed to help us."

Joanna nodded as Caroline ran over to her niece, who was staring out at the ice before her with trepidation. She was the youngest of the bunch, her eagerness at not being left behind clearly at odds with her nervousness over sliding across the ice.

"Come," Caroline called to Joanna, a gleam in her eye, and Joanna wondered now whether her plan had perhaps been too malicious, if she was bringing out the worst in her friend.

But Caroline was on a mission now, and there would be no stopping her. All Joanna could do was go along.

They left the path and the skaters behind as they began to make their way through the deeper snow, lifting one boot after the other, leaving footprints in their wake.

"Are you sure this will work?" Caroline asked, looking back to Joanna.

"No," Joanna said with a laugh and a shake of her head, "but we can do our best."

They hunkered down behind a row of bushes, and quickly went to work packing the snow into hard balls. They had just finished stockpiling their ammunition when voices came from the other side.

"She said Caro was through here," Lord Elijah was saying, and Joanna looked to Caroline, trying to signal with the widening of her eyes and a shrug that she had no idea who might be with him. There was a huff of breath and the crack of a branch through the still of the air. "She said she was in trouble — that she fell. Perhaps—"

Just as he crested the top of the hill, Caroline picked up a ball of snow, stepped back, and heaved it in the air toward him.

And missed.

"What in the—" Lord Elijah's head whipped toward them, but Joanna was there to correct Caroline's mistake.

She leaned back, put everything she had into it, and chucked the ball toward him. She hit him square in the face.

Lord Elijah stood there for a moment in shock as the snow dripped off his handsome, sculpted cheekbones.

Joanna remained immobile for a moment, suddenly completely unsure of this plan, for she had no idea how he was going to react.

"Eli?" Lord Alexander was there next to him, his own mouth open, aghast at what he had just witnessed. He craned his neck to try to see who was there through the trees, and Joanna was reminded of how like Lord Elijah he looked, yet how different as well. Same dark skin tone, same chocolate eyes, same slight curl to his hair — and yet he was slimmer, taller, carried himself with more sleekness than Elijah did, reminding Joanna of a cat.

Then her focus returned to Lord Elijah, and she was struck by the confusion that crossed his face. He looked from one side to the next, taking in his surroundings, before his focus zeroed in on where the assault had come from.

Then just as suddenly he was charging toward them, his gaze fixed, his eyes narrowed, and Caroline let out a squeak before she grabbed Joanna's hand and began pulling her deeper into the trees.

"This was a bad idea!" she called over her shoulder as Lord Elijah thundered through the brush behind them, Lord Alexander calling his name as he must have been in chase.

"I think we should have held our ground," Joanna said, her breath coming in huffs. "We had all of our snowballs back there."

"Yes, but he's much stronger. And faster. And used to fighting."

Joanna stopped so suddenly that her grip freed from

Caroline's and the two of them nearly went flying into the snow together.

"That's it," Joanna said, "he thinks he's back at war."

"What?" Caroline said, turning to her.

"I think the snowball in the face must have brought back some kind of war memory."

Which made sense. If one was used to being targeted with bullets, then it would be difficult to suddenly realize the difference in ammunition.

"Lord Elijah!" she said, holding up her hands in front of her as he came running through the brush. "Elijah!"

He nearly ran her over, but came to an abrupt halt just in time.

"Miss Merryton?" he said, his brow furrowed. "What are you doing here?"

"We're at your home," she said, biting her lip, worried now that there was more wrong than a simple recollection. "Where do you think we are?"

"We're… that is, I'm—"

He looked around helplessly, his eyes wild before they finally settled upon her, and Joanna could tell the moment they recognized her and settled into more peacefulness.

"What's happening?" he asked, his voice nearly breaking with the words, as though it hurt him to have to ask.

"We are part of a Christmas party," she said softly, so that no one else could hear, lest it embarrass him to have to be so explained to. "We are walking and skating, and Caroline and I lured you away so that we could hit you with snowballs."

It sounded so immature, so ridiculous now that she said it aloud, the prank as bad as any that he had played on her.

"We thought it would be a bit of fun, a way to get back at you for your own pranks — and the trouble you got poor Thatcher into last night. But it appears we were wrong."

"No," he said, a guard coming over his face as his jaw

tightened, "it's fine. Of course I know where we are. And as for your scheme..." he paused, then reached down and began packing snow into a ball of his own. He grinned wolfishly, as though there had been no issue, as though all was right and fine in the world.

"You'd better run."

* * *

ELIJAH CRASHED THROUGH THE BUSH, chasing his sister and Miss Merryton, his arms full of the pack of snowballs they had so conveniently created for him. He told his brother to pick up the rest he hadn't been able to carry. Alex had paused for a moment, as though uncertain of whether he should take part in this, but Elijah knew the moment he had relented, when that smile of old had crossed his face, the smile that told him he was interested and willing to join in whatever scheme had arisen.

Now it seemed like Elijah was soaring, even as his boots broke through the deep snow, which began to fill them and melt around his toes. It had been so long since he had done anything fun like this, since he had felt like himself.

He was back to the Elijah of old.

Yes, there had been a moment there where he had been taken back to the battlefield, when he had completely forgotten where he was and who he was with.

He had been hoping for so long that it would all go away, that he would return to the man he was before, but he kept finding memories vanished, moments blurred.

Right now, however, he let that all fall away as he chased after the women, who he was slowly catching up to, hampered as they were by their long skirts and pelisses.

"Catch Caroline!" he yelled to his brother as he took off after Miss Merryton. He lifted a snowball and threw it toward her — not hard enough to cause any hurt, but enough to make it across the expanse toward her. It hit her square in the back, with just enough force to knock her off balance and she went flying into the snow with a yelp.

"Oh, bollocks," he muttered as he ran over to make sure she was not harmed. For a moment, he had forgotten his own strength. "Miss Merryton?" he called out. "I'm sorry, are you all right? I didn't mean—"

But just as he reached her, placing a hand on her back to turn her over and check that all was fine, she whipped around, mitts full of snow, and crushed it into his face.

Elijah stood, clapping his hands to his cheeks at the shock of the frozen wetness, and Miss Merryton jumped in the air, a fist raised in triumph.

"Got you!" she crowed, and from his prone position he looked up at her celebration and acted before he could even think of whether or not he should. In one motion he stood and stepped over, bringing his arms around her and tackling her to the ground.

She gave a little scream as she wiggled around to get out of his grip, and the two of them wrestled in the snow for a moment, each with hands full of snow.

Then her backside snuggled right into the very place where he had been longing for her since that attempted kiss last night, and he stopped fighting altogether as he closed his eyes and tried to will away all temptation.

Which was when she threw an entire handful of snow right down his spine.

It was enough to release her, as the snow began to melt and trickle down his back, rivulets that quite literally cooled his ardor and yet, at the same time, made him want her all the more.

Her hands were on her hips as she stared at him, her eyes

glowing in triumph still, a warrior woman who had, he must admit, bested him.

Despite his promise to stay as far away from her as possible after his attempted-kiss-gone-wrong last night, he wanted nothing more than to step over and caress that smug smile right off her face.

He likely would have tried, had Caroline and Alex not appeared seconds before he did so.

"Did you catch her?" Alex asked, and from the absence of his hat and the wetness on his face, it looked his brother hadn't had any more luck than he had.

"Sort of," Elijah said, and Miss Merryton rolled her eyes.

"How does it feel?" she asked.

"Pardon me?"

"How does it feel to be the one on the other end of such a scheme?" She pointed a finger at him. "I do hope you have learned your lesson."

He lifted an eyebrow. "Do you now?"

"I do."

"Would you like me to show you exactly what I have learned?"

He stepped toward her and he saw her eyes widen, just as Alex cleared his throat from behind him.

"Eli?"

"Yes?" he said, whipping around, finding his siblings both staring at him disapprovingly. He swallowed his next words. "Right. We should return then, shouldn't we?"

"We should," Caroline responded wryly, then looked back and forth between her brothers. "But first, I have something to ask of the two of you."

"Right now?" Elijah said, suddenly quite aware of the need to change both his boots, his shirt, and his companions.

"Yes, right now," Caroline said, looking furtively from

side to side as though someone might be listening to them. "It is one of the only times we will find ourselves alone."

"Very well."

"Leave Thatcher alone," she said, looking at them imploringly. "He's done nothing wrong, I promise you, and I would hate for him to lose his position because of me."

"I talked to Father," Elijah said gruffly, aware that the discontent was his own doing.

"Yes, but that has only led to him and Mother being more watchful of Thatcher. And of me," she said, dipping her head slightly. "Did you not notice that he didn't accompany us this afternoon?'

"Is there something to *be* watchful of, Caro?" Alex asked, lifting an eyebrow as he studied his sister carefully.

Elijah shifted uncomfortably from one foot to the other — and it wasn't because of his soggy boots. "You have to be careful, Caroline," he said, trying to choose his words carefully so she wouldn't become upset with him. "If anyone outside of the family was to find out about the two of you… you could be ruined."

She whipped her head toward him, her chin held high. "I don't care. For I love him."

Elijah felt his jaw go slack upon hearing her words, but he didn't overly care.

"You what?"

"I love him," she said stoically. "And we are going to find a way to be together."

Elijah looked over at Miss Merryton for her reaction, but it seemed that she was already well aware of the news.

Alex was already shaking his head.

"Caroline…" Elijah began, uncomfortable already for this was not something he would typically speak to his sister about, but knew that he had to, for he couldn't let their parents — or Baxter — know more of this. "How do you see that working? He's a servant in our house. Are you going to be married to the man who serves our family dinner?"

"We would leave," Caroline said, strength in her voice, and Elijah didn't doubt that she meant every word she said. "We will look after ourselves."

"What are you going to do, Caro," Alex asked slightly snidely, "become a maid yourself?"

"I don't know yet," she said, her defiance cracking slightly at the question. "I haven't thought it all through yet. Perhaps…" she looked to her friend, "perhaps I will become a seamstress like Joanna."

Alex snorted but turned it into a cough. Elijah wasn't quite so circumspect.

"Caroline," he said with a sigh, "you cannot sew."

"I can!"

Even Joanna was biting her lip, her eyes incredulous.

"Caro," she said gently, stepping toward her, "I didn't realize quite how serious this was."

"It is," she said, blinking, and at the sign of tears, Elijah knew they needed to end this conversation and return to the others — quickly.

"We promise not to do anything to get Thatcher fired," he said. "Is that fair?"

She nodded, clearing her throat.

"Yes. For now, at least. Thank you."

"Now come," he said. "We've some skating to do."

CHAPTER 6

*J*oanna stared at herself in the oval mirror of the vanity, tilting her head to better study her appearance, wondering what Elijah thought when he looked at her now.

And wishing that she didn't care.

She had grown into her pudginess, most of it having become curves instead, thank goodness. Her cheeks were reddened from today's exertions in the snow — exertions that made her further blush just thinking of them.

She wished that her tussle with Elijah hadn't caused her to be so affected. It really shouldn't — not at all. She despised him, she reminded herself. He had caused her such ridicule in their youth, and it didn't seem like he had changed much. He still apparently took great joy in causing trouble, even if it came at the expense of another.

And he hadn't exactly been overly supportive of Caroline and her affections for Thatcher.

The worst of it was, Joanna's own upbringing wasn't that much different from what a footman's likely would be. Yes, she had some noble blood, and had been fortunate enough to be raised in some comfort, but she worked for her living now as much as any servant of this house did. In fact, if it wasn't for her friendship with Caroline, she would have more in common with the housemaids than she did with the ladies.

As evidenced by the dresses she now had to choose from.

She moved away from the image of herself in her chemise and unlaced stays, as she attempted to decide which dress in her dwindling wardrobe she would choose for this evening.

She was saving the one dress for Christmas, of course, which was in just a couple of days, but for tonight, she selected a cream dress with red netting overtop of it. She could re-wear it another day with a red dress beneath, or a spencer overtop, and maybe no one would notice the repeated garment.

There was a knock on the door, and she crossed over to it, opening it with a smile as she expected Caroline's lady's maid, Mary, who helped her dress as Joanna didn't have a maid of her own.

She was wrong.

"Lord Elijah!" she exclaimed, swinging the door half-shut to step behind it so that he couldn't see her in her state of undress, the clasps at the back of the bodice hanging open, as were the laces of her stays. "What are you doing? You can't be here right now!"

"Why not? Do you have company?" he asked with a wink, peering around the doorway to look within.

She narrowed her eyes at him. "I think you are well aware of what the answers are to both of those questions," she said. "I am waiting for a lady's maid, and I'm certainly not in any state of dress to entertain a male guest. Not that he should be here in the first place."

He shrugged, unaffected at her response, and stepped in past her, leaving her staring at him, aghast. Did the man have no qualms whatsoever?

"This is not one of the rooms in this house in which you can come and go as you please!"

He ignored her once more, and she could do nothing more than sigh in frustration as she studied him, hands on her hips. If only he didn't cut such a dashing figure. If only she wasn't secretly stirred by that hint of mischievousness that always followed him around. If only he didn't make her laugh, despite how equally often he angered her.

She crossed her arms over her chest in an attempt to cover the skin over her bodice. "What can I do for you?"

"I needed to talk to you about Caroline," he said, rubbing his forehead. "I know I am supposed to stay away from you, and I will, I promise, but no one else knows about Thatcher except for Alex, and his only suggestion is to force Caro to make a choice, one way or another, by letting all find out about the two of them. I figured you would be far more sensible."

"I can attempt to help," she said cautiously, careful not to commit to anything that might hurt her friend. "What are you thinking?"

"I am thinking that Caroline is being blinded by some unknown infatuation for the man," he said, and then, apparently sensing her discontent, waved a hand around in a spinning motion. "Here, let me help you dress."

"Absolutely not!"

"At least if someone does come in, you will be fastened."

Joanna knew he was making sense, for once, but that didn't mean she enjoyed the idea any more than she should.

"Fine," she said, turning around.

"Hold your hair up," he said, and she brushed it to the side. She had been waiting for the lady's maid to see if she could do something with it to make it look somewhat presentable — or better than its usual limp, straight strands at any rate.

She clenched her teeth together as she tried to push away the tremor that came from the softest brush of his fingers upon the skin of her back as he laced up her stays, from the whisper of his breath upon the back of her neck as he began to slowly push each hook through its eye on the cream dress she would wear beneath the netting.

"Now," he said, and she couldn't help but close her eyes at his voice, so close to her ear. Why did it have to be so deep, so vibrant, so spine-tingling? "Caroline says she is in love. Do you believe it?"

"I can't say that I'm entirely sure," she said with all honesty. "I've hardly seen the two of them together but for the supper when you brought the attention of all to them."

He didn't say anything to that, although she could have sworn she felt rather than heard a low grumble from deep in his chest.

"I've apologized."

"You do a lot of apologizing," she couldn't help but remark, in part to warn him off, and in part to remind herself of who he was and what he had done.

"So it seems," he said, stepping away from her for a moment, and as she was about to turn around and tell him to leave, he slipped the netted dress over her head, the whoosh of fine fabric and his nearness causing every nerve to tingle.

"There," he said, pulling it down as he patted it in place around her. He took a step to the side, bringing her with him so that she could see herself in the mirror, with him standing over her shoulder, his head close to hers. "Perfect."

Joanna watched her eyes widen in the mirror, taking in his words, as well as the picture of them side by side.

"Far from perfect," she said, although even she had no idea whether she was referring to herself, or to the two of them together.

On the outside, he *was* perfection. All sculpted cheekbones and dark features; but the man inside had terrorized her — a fact she must not forget.

"You're still upset." His eyes met hers in the mirror. "I thought you received your revenge in the snow today."

She lifted her chin higher. "That was for Caro."

"Ah yes, my sister, who doesn't seem to have any issue throwing her life away for a footman."

Joanna whirled around at that, hot once more at how flippantly he said such words.

"I'm not much more than a servant myself, you know."

"Joanna," he said, tilting his head. "I can call you Joanna, as we've known one another so long?" He didn't wait for her response, which most assuredly would have been in the negative. "You are the granddaughter of a viscount."

"That hasn't accounted for much," she said, placing her hands on her hips, refusing to allow him to feel sorry for her. "Now tell me," she said, desperate to speak of something else, "what happened today?"

"What do you mean?" he asked, turning, his hand rubbing against his lips as though by covering his mouth he could stop anything he might be tempted to say.

"Today, when you were hit by the snowball," she said, peering at him more closely. "For a moment, it seemed like you didn't know where you were, that you had been taken somewhere else."

"That's ridiculous," he said, snorting, his hand rubbing his forehead, however, in a sign that he was not entirely at ease. "Of course I knew where I was. I have lived at Briercrest Manor nearly my entire life. I know those fields better than any others. I grew up in them. I was merely stunned, that is all, that a woman would succumb to such violence."

So he wanted to avoid the subject. Fine.

It was her turn to raise an eyebrow. "Violence, is it? I would call it retribution."

But it was the violence that had lost him for that moment. Even now, uneasiness swam in his eyes, and Joanna wasn't sure if she was better to press on in asking him to reveal more, or if it would be best to leave it be.

"You must have faced many horrors over there, my lord," she said, softly, gently, trustingly.

"Call me Elijah. And I did," he grunted uncharacteristically. "But no more than any other man."

And suddenly Joanna hated the war viciously, of all that it was, all that it held, that it could take a man like Elijah, who was so full of life and vitality — as mischievous as it was — and turn him into a man that became closed off at even the slightest notion of sharing some idea of his experience with her.

"Leave your hair down," he said suddenly, his eyes running over her now, assessing, attracting.

"Down?" she responded with surprise. "I couldn't."

"Why not?" he asked.

"Well… it just isn't done."

"Says who?" he challenged, his eyes glinting as they narrowed.

"Says everyone."

Her response was thin, but she couldn't think of anything else. And it was the truth.

He reached out ever so slowly, as though waiting for her to knock his hand away. She should. She really should. But that part of her — the part that seemed to be continually betraying her — waited for him to touch her. Longed for him to touch her.

But it was a tease. He stroked one strand of her hair and said only, "Well, then, leave this one down for me, will you?"

And with a wink, he was gone.

Joanna tried to forget his comment about her hair, but when the maid finally arrived, quite surprised and impressed to find that Joanna had succeeded in dressing herself — "but how did you tie the stays, miss?" she had questioned with wide eyes — she had asked if there were any style Joanna preferred.

Joanna had hesitated, finally telling the maid to do as she pleased.

But when she left, she couldn't help but draw one tendril from its pin, allowing it to fall next to her face.

It was only because Elijah's suggestion was likely a preference held by most, she told herself.

That was all.

Even though it wasn't.

She had just descended the staircase when Ophelia cried out from the adjoining room, "It's time for the Yule log!" and Joanna stepped back as the front doors opened wide and two of the footmen — including Thatcher, who was quite obviously keeping his gaze to the floor and not anywhere near Caroline — entered carrying the felled tree. Joanna followed them into the drawing room, where they heaved it into the fireplace that must have been emptied shortly before. A bit of light still filtered in through the white, icy windows, but already a slight chill had entered the room, although Joanna wasn't sure whether or not it was due to the *idea* of an empty fireplace or the actual absence of heat.

The Kentmore family gathered around it first, with their guests to the outside. All took turns sprinkling the log with oil, salt, and wine, each person invited to say a prayer as he or she did so.

Caroline turned and held out a hand to Joanna, who tried to shake her head, but Caroline insisted more firmly, placing the cup of wine in her hand.

"Say your prayer," she commanded, and Joanna nodded dutifully, pouring the wine on the log as she closed her eyes for a moment.

She said a quick prayer for peace and prosperity for all who were here with her this evening. That should be more than a big-enough ask, she reasoned.

But she couldn't help the small part of herself that had one more thing to ask for, something she didn't entirely deserve yet she couldn't help but wish for anyway.

Please Lord, she prayed, *bring me love this Christmas.*

It meant nothing that she met Elijah's eyes when she opened her own.

For he was the last man she would ever — *should* ever — fall in love with.

So why did his wink cause her heart to flip?

She was going to have to get a handle on herself, she reasoned. Or she would be in for humiliation once more.

Humiliation she had vowed to avoid for the rest of her life.

CHAPTER 7

Elijah had spent most of his life lacking any real purpose.

He had gone to school, yes. He had joined the army, yes.

But at that point in time, he hadn't particularly cared about what he was doing. He went through the motions because it was expected of him, but he'd never actually worked incredibly hard in excelling or in proving himself to even be worthy.

Because what did it matter?

He would always be the second son of a marquess, who wasn't good for anything, really — not even in standing in line for the title anymore, not now that Baxter had sons.

He would have made a terrible marquess, anyway. For he lacked commitment. He lacked responsibility. He lacked purpose.

Until now.

Now he was determined that there was one thing — or one person — who was going to change all of that.

For he wanted Joanna Merryton.

MERRY MISRULE

All he had to do was convince her that he was not the man she thought he was.

And he wasn't. Not really. The Elijah Kentmore that had left for the war years ago had been killed along with dozens of others on the fields of Salamanca.

The man who stood in his place now was but a shadow of who he had been before.

A shadow lacking memories, recognition, time.

One thing he could not forget, however, was the image in his head of Joanna half-dressed. Nor the sight of his fingers, so rough and undainty, upon the soft, pale skin of her back. Nor the reflection of the two of them, staring back from the mirror.

This Christmas he would win Joanna over. He had no idea how just yet. He could only wish that it was *her* memories of the past that were erased, for then it might be much easier for her to give him a chance.

But that was a lie — for he would never wish this upon anyone, least of all her.

He watched her enter the drawing room, slightly hesitant, unsure, and he longed to go to her and offer his arm, to help her acclimate to all of these people who were part of his friends and family, but who seemed so distant since his return.

But to do so would quite contravene his promise to her to stay far away, and so instead he followed her with his eyes — until he saw that Alex took the very place he had wished for himself.

Suddenly, his brother, the man who had always been his partner in everything they did, who he had always so wanted to be like to the point of joining the army, became his opponent.

His attention was caught by his elder brother across the room, where Baxter and Ophelia were holding court as though they were king and queen of their castle, which he supposed they were, in a sense. And yet, still, it grated on him, especially when his parents were still here, and should be filling that role themselves.

Elijah had an idea.

An idea that would solve both of his immediate annoyances.

He made his way across the room, sidling up next to his brother.

"Alex, Miss Merryton," he said, taking a sip of his drink as he greeted the pair, keeping his voice light. "I have an idea."

Alex turned to him, one brow quirked, although he couldn't mask the interested gleam in his eye.

"Oh?"

Eli tilted his head over toward Baxter and Ophelia. "It's about the two of them. They're a bit high on their thrones, don't you think?"

"Well," Alex said as he shrugged, "that's kind of the way of it now. You've been gone for some time, Eli, and Baxter *will* be the next marquess."

"But he's not yet," Elijah said with a grin, "so what do you suppose we have some fun with him while we still can?"

Alex's eyes glinted.

Elijah didn't care so much about what Alex thought, however. He stole a glance at Joanna, who was eyeing him with interest, for which he breathed a big sigh of relief. He knew he should be trying to prove to her that he had matured, yet he couldn't help but try to have some fun and liven this party up a bit.

"What are you thinking?" Alex finally asked.

"Well…" Elijah said, already laughing, "you know how Baxter likes to make a long, drawn-out toast at every dinner?"

"Of course," Alex said.

"I have an idea on how we could make his toast a little more interesting this evening."

Alex eyed him doubtfully, but nodded for him to continue.

"I'll need a little help," Elijah said, and then outlined his plan. Alex grinned with delight at the thought, while Joanna seemed skeptical, but intrigued at how it might all play out. "Now, we must wait."

So wait they did. Elijah was hoping that Alex would find somewhere else to take his interest, but he seemed just as curious by Joanna and her newfound beauty as Elijah was. He couldn't blame his brother, but nor did he feel like competing with him. For Alex would win. He always did.

When the dinner hour came, he found himself on one side of Joanna, Alex on the other.

As though on cue, Baxter stood, glass in hand.

Elijah kept his eye on that glass, hoping that Thatcher had carried out his task as he had requested.

"Good evening, my friends," Baxter said, his glass small in his large fingers. His smile stretched wide in his heavily jowled face, so unlike his brothers in looks and stature. "My family and I would like to thank you all for being here."

He continued on for a couple of minutes, speaking about nothing at all, before lifting his hand, and Elijah sat up straighter.

"Now, a toast, to all of you — the best wine that we have to offer. Here is to the greatest Christmas celebration in all of England!"

He lifted his glass, while the rest of them did so with their wine as well. Then Baxter took a big swig of his drink — and started sputtering.

"What in the devil is this?" he snarled, staring at the glass as though it had conjured itself into a different liquid. "This is... why this is—"

"Absolutely lovely," Ophelia cut in, a hand on his arm as she leaned forward, her smile forced and obviously intending to be contagious. Baxter, however, did not seem to understand.

"You!" he pointed to Thatcher. "Come here."

Thatcher obeyed. Baxter leaned in and muttered something in his ear. Thatcher nodded and walked away.

"My apologies, all," he said with a low, sweeping bow. "This is not the drink I expected. We shall have all of the port cleared immediately."

A low rumbling began around the table, and Elijah hurriedly tossed his drink back.

"It's fine, Bax," Alex said, leaning forward. "It tastes as excellent as ever."

"Are you daft?" Baxter said incredulously. "I don't know what this is supposed to be, but it most certainly isn't fit to drink."

Elijah choked back his laughter and reached out a hand.

"May I?"

Baxter nodded and Elijah took the glass and tasted.

"Baxter," he said, looking at him with a tilted head, "it's water."

And at that, the rest of the table dissolved into laughter. Alex clapped Elijah on the shoulder, but Elijah didn't even look over. For what mattered most? Joanna.

He turned, but saw her head was dipped, the smile he was sure was on her face hidden.

When she finally looked up at him, he didn't like what he saw. She seemed disappointed. And he realized then that he had done nothing but continue down the path she had expected him to take. The path away from her.

* * *

Elijah stared across the room.

Every time he thought he was making some kind of progress with Joanna, he seemed to be pushed backward. He had thought she enjoyed his joke, but apparently, he was wrong. It had been too cruel, she had murmured, and after it, she hadn't spoken to him throughout the entirety of dinner. Should he leave things where they were or take it a step further?

Probably leave it.

But Elijah had never exactly been known for doing what he was supposed to do, the thing that would be rational.

One of the women, Lady Ox something or other, had sat down at the piano and was beginning to tinkle away a Christmas tune that he thought had something to do with greenery, although he couldn't be entirely sure. His parents took to the dance floor, followed by the admiral and his wife, and then Lord Cristobel approached Caroline, who reluctantly took his hand with a forlorn look back at the doorway, where Thatcher was, of course, standing sentry, waiting to be required.

Elijah saw Alex take a step toward Joanna. He should let them dance together. She would surely prefer him, and Alex would be a much better man for her than Elijah would ever be.

He was always out for himself first. For a good laugh, for attention, for fun.

Which was why he did what he did, and cut in first.

"Joanna," he said with a nod to her, "may I have this dance?"

"No," she said firmly, setting her jaw, and he looked down into her eyes with supplication.

"I promise to be on my best behavior," he said, hoping she could read his true intentions. "Please?"

"Very well," she sighed, although she looked from side to

side as though hoping someone would come rescue her. But tonight, he was going to be her savior instead of her foe.

He took her hand in his, leading her toward the middle of the dance floor, taking great joy in placing one hand on her waist and taking her gloved hand in the other. The netting of her dress caused friction against his hand, every inch of his skin already sensitive to her touch.

He couldn't say what it was about her that was causing him to be as drawn to her as a gift on Christmas morning. A gift he could hardly wait to unwrap.

He could already imagine what she would look like. All delicious curves, soft skin, with that captivating mouth on top like a bow, a mouth that would say exactly what she thought.

She was beautiful, yes. She was dewy skin and high cheekbones and chocolate tresses.

She was also very firm that she wanted nothing to do with him. He had an innate need to prove her wrong, to show her that he could be the man she never knew she needed.

It wouldn't be easy. For there was the knowing behind her eyes, the way she watched others, the fact that she was different from every other woman of his acquaintance.

She hadn't lived the easiest life, and yet she found joy in it all the same.

"What are you thinking about?" she asked, looking up at him, her eyes squinted slightly, and he wondered if they were narrowed in question or if she actually couldn't see him altogether very well.

"Nothing," he answered, his response rote and immediate, and then he decided to be honest rather than polite. "Actually, that isn't altogether true."

"No?"

"I'm thinking about just what is so alluring about you."

Her eyes widened at his clearly unexpected answer. "That's not exactly a word most would use to describe me."

"Then most are wrong."

"Is this another trick?" she tilted her head to the side as he led her around the room, the scents of the evergreen and holly — and jasmine that had teased his senses as he had helped dress her — floating up to him, causing him to become quite heady with it all.

"Not a trick." He shook his head. "I promised no more tricks."

She quirked an eyebrow. "What was that then, a few minutes ago, with your brother?"

"No more tricks against *you*," he amended. "Only to those who deserve them. Besides, you were intrigued."

She dipped her head. "I know. But I was wrong. It went too far."

"You're right." He sighed, for she was. He had thought it would be a bit of fun, but when he had seen the embarrassment on Baxter's face, it hadn't been worth it any longer.

"And I don't know if I would call that much in line with the Christmas spirit."

He snorted. "Christmas spirit. What is that even supposed to mean?"

He hadn't meant for anything to come across with the remark, but he could tell that she sensed his unease all the same.

"Christmas spirit? Why, it's... it's the entire feeling of Christmas. The love that surrounds it, the sense that all is right in the world, the gifts, the fact that it was on this day a savior was born into the world."

He searched her face, sensing the sincerity in her words.

"How can you say that, when you have lost so much yourself?"

She smiled somewhat self-consciously. "I haven't lost

much at all. My grandmother, yes, and I miss her nearly every day. But I was so fortunate to spend as much time with her as I did to learn from her about love and life and everything it holds. My parents were who they were, and the fact that my father didn't want me, well, that says more about him than it does about me. I was but a child."

The thought of someone rejecting her, no matter her age, caused a stirring deep within Elijah — a stirring to show her that she didn't deserve such rejection at all, and that she should never feel it again by another.

"That's more reasonable than most would consider."

"I am more reasonable than most."

He chuckled wryly. "Especially me," he said, reading into her words.

"Especially you," she agreed, and now his laugh was much louder, enough to draw the attention of a few of the couples around them.

The stares continued, and suddenly he realized that Lady Oxford — right, Oxford, that was her name — had finished her song but they were still stepping and swaying in time to the music that was but an echo around them.

Elijah cleared his throat and stepped back away from Joanna. "Thank you for the dance."

"Thank you."

"Oh, and Joanna?"

"Yes?"

"Your hair is beautiful tonight."

Before she could respond, Alex was there, claiming her hand for the next set.

Elijah could do nothing but sigh and turn away.

He was going to have to take things one step further if he wanted to win her hand.

And win her hand he would.

CHAPTER 8

*E*very Christmas morning, Joanna woke with the same wonder and excitement as she had when she was a child, when her grandmother would have presents awaiting her, left there by the enigma that was Saint Nicholas.

When she had been old enough to understand that Saint Nicholas was, in fact, someone much dearer to her, she had only become more appreciative of what her grandmother had done for her.

But she had been telling the truth when she had shared with Elijah of how much she missed her. Even the Christmases she was entirely alone, doing nothing but reading a good book by the fire, going to the church service, and dining with friends, she still looked forward to all that the day held.

She grinned today when she opened the wardrobe, as the dress that had held the place of honor in the very middle was finally her selection. It wasn't one she would normally wear in the morning, but after breakfast they would go into the village for the Christmas church service before returning for the feast.

And a feast it would be. Joanna recalled the few Christmases she had spent here in the past, and they always required her to loosen her stays.

She bit her lip, remembering the teasing that had followed. She had been quite plump in her youth, and it had only been over the past few years that she had grown into her curves.

Besides her grandmother, she had exchanged Christmas gifts with but one other person — Caroline. She couldn't wait until the day she would be able to choose or create something for her own children. If that day ever came.

But no matter. Today was Christmas, and it was a day to celebrate.

"Joanna!"

Joanna turned to see that Caroline had her door open a crack, and was waving her in.

"Were you watching for me?" she asked as she opened the door and entered Caroline's room. It was sumptuous, romantic, just like Caroline herself. The walls were delicate rose pink, the canopies a darker shade somewhere between pink and red, with tiny rosebuds embroidered on them.

"I was," Caroline said, shutting the door behind her. She wore a silk emerald dress with tiny red flowers tucked into her chignon, a look that would have made Joanna look childlike, but was charmingly elegant on Caroline. "Happy Christmas, Joanna."

"Happy Christmas, Caroline."

Caroline reached out and Joanna embraced her, grateful that, if nothing else, this long friendship had already stood the test of many trials that had come their way.

The daughter of a marquess typically did not invite a seamstress for a Christmas party. But Caroline didn't see people by their station or profession. She saw them for who they truly were, and Joanna loved her for it.

And she would support Caroline in whatever she chose to do with her life.

Caroline squeezed her hands as she released her, before walking over to the wardrobe in the corner, opening the door and searching within, emerging with a small package.

"This is for you."

She held it out to her, and Joanna smiled at her before opening it, trying not to allow herself too much excitement.

But she couldn't help it. She did not receive many gifts, and she looked forward to Caroline's gift to her every year — even when they had been apart.

"Oh, Caroline," she said, as she lifted the necklace out of the paper it was wrapped in. "It's beautiful."

"I saw it and thought of you," Caroline said, reaching for it and bringing the ends around Joanna's neck before fastening the clasp. "Red is so beautiful on you."

Joanna beamed at her as she walked over to the long oval mirror in the corner of Caroline's room, admiring herself in the glass.

"Thank you, Caroline," she said. "I've never had anything like it before. It's too much, but I shall accept it all the same for it's too beautiful to refuse."

It truly was. It was a small ruby, inlaid into a gold square, laced onto a gold chain. She could hardly stop from touching it and looking at how it lay perfectly on her chest. She tore herself away to walk over to the bed, upon which she had laid the paper-wrapped package she had brought with her.

She picked it up and passed it to Caroline. "This is for you."

"Oh, Joanna," she said, "you didn't have to."

She always said that.

"I wanted to."

"Well, thank you," she said, before unwrapping the paper, allowing creamy fabric to fall out of it.

"It's gorgeous," Caroline breathed, allowing the fabric to float over her fingers. "Did you make this?"

"I did."

Joanna could never afford to buy anything that would be worthy of a gift for Caroline, but she could create something for her instead.

"I can hardly wait to don it," she said, before her eyes flickered up to Joanna with a gleam. "I actually have the perfect place to wear it."

"Oh?"

"Joanna, I need to tell you something, but you must promise that you won't say anything to anyone."

Joanna hesitated, having an idea of what Caroline might want to tell her, unsure if she should make such a promise.

"Caro, I'm not sure—"

"Please, Joanna?"

"Of course." She softened, unable to deny her request.

"Samuel gave me my Christmas gift last night."

"Samuel?"

"Thatcher," she said, her face dissolving into a smile. "Samuel is his given name."

"Oh, that's right," she said, before offering an encouraging expression. "What did he give you?"

She walked back to the wardrobe, this time emerging with a small pouch. She fit two fingers inside, before slipping something onto her finger.

"Look," she breathed.

It was a small, gold band, thin but beautiful in its own way. She looked up, meeting Caroline's eager, hopeful grin.

"Did he…" Joanna began, not wanting to ask anything that might cause Caroline to become upset if he hadn't, but needing to know.

MERRY MISRULE

"Yes!" Caroline squealed. "He asked me to marry him. The ring was his mother's."

"Oh, Caroline," Joanna said, her voice infused with awe. "I'm so happy for you."

She gave Caroline another hug, even as a bit of trepidation filled her — not at Caroline's choice in life, for she knew better than anyone that happiness had many different forms, and it did not always include marrying the highest title or into the greatest wealth. No, what worried her was what Caroline's family's reaction would be, and what they might do when they learned of her plans. She could envision them crushing Caroline's happiness, and she didn't want to see it in action.

"Thank you, Jo," Caroline said as she released her. "Now I have to ask you another favor."

"Of course."

"We haven't yet planned exactly when or how we will be married, but we are aware that my family will likely not be thrilled with the idea."

Joanna bit her lip. That was something of an understatement.

"We may decide to try to marry without their knowledge."

"Oh, Caroline," she said, "how would you do so?"

"I'm not sure yet," Caroline replied. "But if I need any help… would you be there for me?"

"Absolutely," Joanna said without resolve. "Anything you need."

As they made their way downstairs for breakfast, she couldn't help but wonder, however, what Elijah would think of the plan, and why it mattered to her what he might think or do. His opinion shouldn't mean anything — it was Caroline's father and Baxter who could cause the most discord.

But she couldn't help how troubled she was that it was Elijah's reaction that would matter the most to her.

* * *

Elijah was excited.

It was a state of being that he had not experienced in quite some time.

But it was Christmas morning, Joanna was here, and he was going to win her affections. He was sure of it. She was currently somewhere down the long table, although he wasn't entirely sure where. He had been relegated to sit near the children, which he supposed was somewhat appropriate, although he wasn't entirely pleased to admit it.

"Christopher," he said to one of Baxter's children, who was sitting on his left. Admiral Cuthbert's wife was on the other side, continuously leaning in toward him. "Are you going to eat your eggs?"

"No," Christopher said with a sigh as he stirred them around his plate. "They are disgusting."

He enunciated each syllable so completely that Elijah nearly laughed, but he knew that it would only embarrass the boy.

"Here," Elijah said, reaching over, beginning to move things around the boy's plate. "The egg is like the lake. Then," he moved the tomatoes, "the pieces of toast are the islands. The tomatoes you can break apart and they are volcanoes. The middle part — the part with the seeds — that's the lava that is coming out."

Christopher was looking at him with rapt admiration, and Elijah began warming to the game.

"Now this — this green stuff, this food for rabbits that has no business being on any of our plates — that is quite obviously the vegetation. The trees nearby. And this—"

Suddenly he realized that Christopher was no longer looking at him. Instead, he was peering down the table. Elijah lifted his gaze and followed where he was looking. Almost the entire table was watching them now, listening to his imaginings.

"Err—" he cleared his throat.

"Elijah," Baxter said, lifting one of his eyebrows, his expression so completely identical to their father's that Elijah would have laughed at any other time, "just what do you think you are teaching my son?"

"Just having a little fun, Baxter," Elijah said with a shrug and a smile. "It's Christmas."

"So when it is not Christmas, do you belong in the nursery with the children, then?"

Elijah knew that Baxter was still smarting from the prank they had pulled on him earlier. But even so, his words still tugged deep in his stomach, reminding him of how he had always lacked the approval of both his father and his eldest brother.

Elijah, always the child. The prankster. The one who couldn't take anything seriously, nor focus on any one responsibility.

Alex hadn't been any different. And yet, somehow, he had always managed to come away from each situation without a blemish on his name.

He looked out of the corner of his eye.

Christopher was eating his island oasis.

Elijah smiled triumphantly. So what if his methods were slightly juvenile? They worked.

He winked at Christopher, who smiled back.

He could only hope that Joanna wouldn't think any less of him.

Elijah had the entire breakfast to wait until he was able to find out.

"Joanna," he called lightly to her as the rest of the party filtered out of the dining room, where they were eating for the occasion instead of in the much smaller breakfast room.

She paused as though unsure of whether or not she should turn around, but finally she looked over her shoulder. She was too good of a person to even pretend to ignore him.

"Yes?"

When she turned to face him, he was nearly speechless. She wore a dress that would have been stunning on its own. Much different from her usual wear, which only served to show the stark difference between her beauty and her garments' drabness, the dress today would have been eye catching standing on a mannequin. The crimson silk was intricately embroidered with tiny diamonds of a crystal blue around the hem and the bodice, drawing his eye down.

For that was the true beauty of the dress — how it looked upon its wearer. It hugged Joanna's every curve until her waist, causing his fingers to twitch with their desire to reach out and follow the silk, to touch where the dress did. From the waist, it flowed out to the ground, but it shifted and stirred with her, accentuating her every movement.

After he was finally able to focus, he noticed that she was looking at him quite strangely — which made complete sense.

"Can I speak to you for a moment?" he finally managed.

She bit her lip in what he hoped was naught but a moment's hesitation, before she nodded and he led her through the dining room and into the drawing room. It was still an open room that would ensure they were not ensconced anywhere that might be deemed inappropriate, yet there was a window seat in an alcove that allowed for more private moments, as he hoped this one would be.

"Is everything all right?" she asked, tilting her head to the side.

"Yes," he said, nodding his head, realizing he was making a mess of all of this. He reached out a hand to the shelf beside him to shift his weight, but encountered pine needles and pulled back his fingers with a wince.

He cursed under his breath and Joanna laughed slightly, lightening the moment and helping him feel much more at ease.

"Joanna…" he began, and she looked at him somewhat questioningly, "I have something for you," he finally blurted out, and her eyes widened.

"For me?"

"Yes," he said, reaching into his inner coat pocket. "I know I shouldn't have and yet… I felt I owed you this."

She reached out and took the small package he offered, the touch of their fingers, even through her soft gloves, causing his to burn. When she dipped her head to open it, he was afforded a view of her beautiful chocolatey silk strands, caught up in their pins, and he longed to release one and allow that silk to flow through his fingers.

But instead, he had to be comfortable with simply taking in his fill.

She opened the package, taking its contents in her hand, staring at it for a moment.

"Do you like it?" he finally had to ask.

"It's… a pocket watch," was all she said, and his heart hurt a bit that she was not overly excited.

"Yes," he said, "to replace the one I caused you to lose so many years ago."

"Thank you," she said, finally looking up to meet his eyes, but he didn't miss the tear in hers. Was it a tear of happiness? Of sadness?

"Did I do something wrong?" he finally had to ask, and she dipped her head once more.

"Yes. No. Oh, Elijah, I know this is coming from a place of care, and I do so appreciate the sentiment."

"But…"

"Well, the pocket watch meant something not because it was a pocket watch but because it belonged to my grandmother. It was one of the only things I had of hers."

"I know, Joanna," he said, remorse filling him anew. "And I'm sorry again. I don't know what to do now, but—"

"Is that a pocket watch?"

Elijah closed his eyes for a moment. Cecily. Wonderful. She was the last person he desired to be here at the moment.

"Yes," Joanna said, setting her chin as she looked up to her. "Lord Elijah is replacing one that I… lost long ago."

"Oh yes," Cecily gushed. "He is quite the giver of pocket watches, is he not? Why, he gave me one once as well!"

And with that she reached into her dress and pulled out a pocket watch that, from the look on Joanna's face, could be none other than the very one that had belonged to her grandmother.

CHAPTER 9

Joanna could only stare with mouth agape.

Her pocket watch — her grandmother's pocket watch — was hanging from Cecily's hand, swinging by its gold chain back-and-forth, back-and-forth, mocking her with its closeness.

It wasn't anything particularly special. It was gold enamel, featuring a bouquet of flowers in the middle of a four-layered border, each one intimately familiar to Joanna.

The outside border was blue, with red and gold crowns inlaid into it.

And on the back, she knew there would be an inscription.

To my love.

It had not been inscribed for her, but her grandmother had told her that the love that filled it continued on through the gift.

Elijah's gift was actually much more elaborate. It was gold, with one central flower encrusted in diamonds.

She didn't want him to think her ungrateful. Truly, she didn't. He had no need to give her anything, and the fact that he had thought of a pocket watch showed that his intentions to make amends were sincere.

It also proved, however, that he didn't actually understand what the value of the watch had been to her.

"Yes," Joanna said now, her voice strangled, "as it happens, I do recognize that watch."

"I must have shown it to you then!"

"You did," Joanna's lips somehow formed a tight smile. "You don't recall where the watch came from?"

"Mm, no, I don't," Cecily said with a bright smile, although a quick darkness passed over her eyes, telling Joanna that she well remembered all that had occurred. "It's a mystery!"

Joanna opened her mouth once more, but suddenly Elijah's hand was on her shoulder.

"I can hardly believe you still have it, Cecily," he said, and when Joanna looked up at him, a protest on her lips, he silently shook his head. "How lovely. Your husband must be thrilled."

Joanna nearly snorted at that, but then Elijah held out an elbow. "Should we go and rejoin the others?"

Joanna nodded, and it wasn't until Cecily left them to fetch her cloak for the walk to the church service that she turned to him with her hands on her hips. She didn't need to demand his explanation, however, for he already had one awaiting her.

"I have a plan," he murmured in her ear. "We won't be able to put it in place until later, but I will get your grandmother's pocket watch back. I promise."

She turned to him then, searching his deep brown eyes, wondering if what he said was true.

"Do you trust me?"

She didn't. Not entirely. But he seemed so earnest, so

committed, that she didn't have it within her to break his spirit.

"Let's give it a try," she said, forcing a smile to her face.

She wasn't sure how he thought to pull this off, but if there was any man she knew could come up with the perfect scheme, it was he.

* * *

Elijah was buoyed by hope. Joanna had, at the very least, not completely turned away from him and shut him down.

He knew she was trying to show pleasure over his gift, even though it had done nothing but cause her additional grief. He had done the best he could, but Cecily showing up with the watch that Joanna actually longed for... well, there was nothing he could have done about that.

But he could get it back for her.

He had a few tricks on how to encourage people to give up things that belonged to them, to scheme them out of the items. He had to be careful, however, for Cecily was already aware that Joanna wanted what she had, and if she were to simply lose the watch, Joanna was sure to be blamed. The fact that she was a seamstress while Cecily was the daughter of an earl and the wife of a viscount, would certainly mean that Joanna would be found in the wrong.

He donned his cloak and hat before opening the door as all who filled Briercrest began to pile into the waiting sleighs. As many of the guests had arrived in one themselves, there were more than enough to fit them all.

He hoped for the chance to sit under one of the warm fur rugs with Joanna pressed up against him, but alas, he was next to the admiral's wife once more.

"Mrs. Cuthbert," he greeted her, and the woman beamed up

at him so hard that her eyes closed. She was near to his mother's age, but he couldn't help note that she wiggled in much closer to him than was necessary. He swallowed, looking for help or an escape, but he was pressed up against the side of the sleigh.

"Lord Elijah," she gushed, so loudly that his ear started to ring. He supposed that when one lived with a near-deaf husband for so many years, one would become used to speaking in so great a volume. "Happy Christmas."

"And to you," he returned politely.

"It is a chilly one today, is it not? Thank goodness we have one another tucked in here under all of these layers."

She laughed, but unfortunately there were not nearly *enough* layers between the two of them. If she came any closer, then he was sure *he* was the one who would be ruined.

He looked up toward the other sleighs which were also being loaded, and found that sitting across from him, watching him with interest, was Joanna.

She was laughing. At him.

He stared back at her, slowly shaking his head at the fact she was taking such pleasure from his obvious distress. That was when she really began to laugh in earnest, so much so that her sleigh companions looked at her with some question. Caroline, who was seated next to her, leaned in and asked something, and when Joanna obviously explained just what had her so entertained, Caroline began to snicker as well.

Elijah shot both of them what he hoped was a dark look, one telling them that they were going to face retribution for their glee.

Just what that would be, he wasn't entirely sure yet.

***

JOANNA HAD QUITE ENJOYED WATCHING Elijah struggle. There was obviously nothing he could do to extricate himself from his position — quite literally — but when the horses had pulled the sleighs into the yard of the Chearsley Parish Church of Saint Nicholas, he had jumped out at nearly a run, holding the church door open for the rest of them.

"Careful, Eli," she murmured as she slipped past him, "some might get the wrong impression."

He snorted as he followed her in, taking the end seat beside her on the pew, with Caroline on her left.

"You're cruel."

"I'm not," she protested, "just having a bit of fun."

"I'm glad one of us enjoyed that," he muttered. "You must protect me on the way home."

"You're a grown man!"

"Even so," he said with a sigh, "it caused me great suffering."

As Joanna rolled her eyes, Christopher went running by them, but Elijah deftly stepped out of the pew and picked him up, fitting him in between him and the edge.

"Just where do you think you are going, young man?" he asked, and the five-year-old turned to him with a grin.

"To see baby Jesus!"

"All in good time," Elijah said. "The minister is coming out now. We must wait until he's finished to go forward."

Christopher heaved a great sigh and Joanna's lips twitched at what categorized such a great tragedy when one was young. How she wished it remained so for her.

"Uncle Eli?" Christopher whispered.

"Yes?"

"Were you there when I was born?"

Elijah started, and Joanna swung her head toward them, interested in just how Elijah was going to handle this conversation.

"Not in the room, no, of course not," he said. "That is no place for a man."

"But were you in the house?"

"I..." Elijah paused, tilting his head as though he had to think on it, "I'm not entirely sure."

"You don't know? I was your first nephew."

"I...I'm sure I was," he said now, although his features had tightened, and Joanna could tell he was not particularly comfortable with the conversation.

Another memory he had apparently lost. What had happened to cause it?

She had no more time to think on it, however, for then the first chords of Joy to the World began to resound from the organ, and she stood along with the rest of the congregation.

It was a beautiful service in the little village chapel. Their house party and Briercrest servants made up three pews, the rest filled with villagers. Joanna appreciated the moment in time of this Christmastide to be in the midst of others who were not marquesses or admirals or heirs to a title or a wife or daughter of one of them. Here, they were just people. People who had come together to celebrate Christmas in its truest form.

Christopher was remarkably well behaved, and his little sister Clementine even took a seat next to them, warming Joanna's heart when she wiggled her way between Elijah and Joanna before taking a seat on Joanna's lap in order to better see the service.

Joanna's heart churned as she wondered, for a moment, whether she would ever have a child of her own. Elijah's face flashed in the role of their father, startling her, for while she could admit that his nearness had awakened the attraction to him that she had always fought against, she had never entertained the thought that she might ever have any sort of emotional connection to him, besides one of anger or avoidance.

But now that the four of them sat here together, like a small family… it tugged at her, and she told herself to fight against it. Elijah was not the kind of man who would make a good husband, nor a good father.

Or would he?

She thought back to breakfast that very morning. She knew that most had disdained Elijah's actions with Christopher, but she had actually been quite entertained. His voice had cut through the others down the table even before all attention had been pointed toward him, and she had been eagerly awaiting to see what else he could come up with.

He was creative, if nothing else, and knew how to entertain a child.

Whether he could be responsible for one, however, was an entirely different question.

After the service was over, they walked up the aisle between the pews, the old wood and musty smell that always came with small, old churches accompanying them, so that the children could see the manger with the little baby Jesus right in the middle.

"He's so small," Christopher said.

"Like me!" Clementine chimed in.

"Yes, just like you," Joanna said with a laugh.

They all stood there for a moment, taking in the scene before them, and Joanna couldn't help but allow her gaze to wander over Elijah once more. His dark hair was curled with a dash of debonair, his eyes laughing as they always were — until they looked up to meet hers, and then they darkened with a sense of knowing, telling her that he understood what she was thinking, and wished for it too.

She shouldn't. He shouldn't. But the air seemed to go out of the room and she wanted nothing more than for this to be real, for him to want her just as assuredly as she wanted him, for reasons beyond all reason.

"Christopher! Clementine!"

Ophelia was calling the children now, beckoning them back out into the crisp winter air, and when Clementine jumped from Joanna's arms, she felt the loss of her presence within them.

"Well," Joanna said, filling the pregnant air that remained as most of the congregation filed out of the church. "We best go."

"Don't forget your promise," Elijah said, one eyebrow quirked.

"My promise?"

"To protect me," he said, before leaning in close. "Do you know how many times Mrs. Cuthbert's hand found its way toward my leg?"

Joanna laughed out loud at that, but Elijah feigned insult.

"It's not funny!" he exclaimed. "I had to keep pushing it back, and I moved so far away I was nearly falling over the side of the sleigh."

"Well, I cannot recall making any such promise."

"Please?" he said, turning in her direction, and she wasn't entirely sure whether his desperation was real or feigned. "I will owe you forever, I promise."

"Here I thought you already did."

"But even more so," he vowed. "Anything you want from me, I will make it so."

"Well..." she said, biting her lip, knowing that she was making a deal with the devil but unable to resist the temptation.

"Very well."

"Excellent." He grinned as they stepped through the door and he swept his hand out toward the sleigh, which only had room for two more, anyway. "Our chariot awaits."

CHAPTER 10

✨

*E*lijah could blame his reaction to Joanna on the fact that it had been quite some time since he had been with a woman. He had been recuperating from his war injury for a few months before he had begun the journey home. Even before then, while he had never been particularly shy around women, he was by no means a rake of any sort.

Of all the women he had met and charmed, he had never responded to a woman the way he did Joanna.

Since he had seen her in the library that first night, he had desired her physically with all of his being.

There was more to it, however. He found himself looking to her every time he made a joke just to see if she would laugh. He wondered what she thought of her meal, contemplated whether or not she fell asleep quickly, was curious about what she spoke of when she was with the women and whether she sewed for fun or if she only did so in order to make a living.

He wanted to know everything about her, and he wanted to be the man that would complement her in every way.

There was one thing he knew without question, he noted

as her frame molded into his from where she sat next to him — they would fit together better than any pair ever had before. He was sure of it.

"Thank you," he said, ensuring to tuck the blanket in more tightly around her. "I am ever in your debt."

"The real question is," she said with a sigh, "just what to use my favor for?"

He quirked up an eyebrow.

"Careful," he warned, "don't use it too quickly. You might come to regret it later."

"I never regret anything," she said quietly. "Every mistake made is something to learn from. You cannot have made a different choice unless you possess the same information that you have after your first decision."

"An interesting thought," he remarked, curious about just how this woman's mind worked.

Joanna began waving then, and he followed her gaze to see that Caroline was whizzing by in the other sleigh. She waved back to the two of them before the sleigh passed, and Elijah suddenly stood, calling out to the footman driving theirs.

"I say, Georges! Beat that sleigh!"

"My lord?" The footman, his nose, ears, and cheeks completely red from the cold, looked at him in shock.

"I said 'Beat that sleigh!' Come Georges, you don't want Thatcher getting the best of us, do you?"

Nor did he want Thatcher out of his sight with his sister in front of him, for his parents and Baxter and Ophelia must be in the third sleigh.

Georges grinned, and without any more encouragement, he urged the horses on, and their sleigh began to pass Thatcher's once more.

"That's it!" Elijah said, standing and shouting triumphantly, one fist in the air.

Thatcher looked over, saw the race was on, and began to prod his own horses forward.

Joanna cried out with glee as she held a hand over her hat, making sure it didn't fly off into the wind. Lord and Lady Oxford were bundled into the sleigh with their son as well, but seemed to be enjoying the race along with them, while Alex urged Georges on himself. Shouts and taunts began to fill the air as they all called out to one another while the sleighs continued forward as fast as the snow allowed.

"To the break in the trees!" Elijah shouted, standing again, unable to help himself. He had always been competitive, and even now, when he had no way to actually affect the win, he couldn't help but put everything he had into this.

Joanna tried to stand, but then fell off balance and into his side, laughing. She held onto his arm, and even through her mittens and his layers of clothing, he enjoyed the feel of her, especially when it meant that he was supporting her.

"Go, go!" she called, until finally they surged ahead and skidded through the break of the trees, coming out first the other side. All within their sleigh let out a shout of glee, and Elijah couldn't help himself.

He leaned down, placed his gloved hands on either side of Joanna's face, and kissed her right on the lips.

It was a quick smack of their lips together, but it obviously surprised them both, as suddenly they sat back and stared at one another.

"I… I'm sorry, I shouldn't have—" he began, knowing that he should never have done such a thing without her permission, but before he could say anything, his voice was overwhelmed by Thatcher and Georges beginning to shout good-naturedly to one another about whether or not the race was fair.

"You started this, you know," Joanna murmured, and he wasn't sure whether or not she was referring to the jovial argument between the two footmen or their own interest in one another.

Either way she was right.

"That I did," he murmured back, looking out over the snowy expanse below them, "that I did."

And he wasn't sorry.

Not one bit.

* * *

Their "small tea" that afternoon was anything but, just like most meals at Briercrest Manor.

Joanna, however, could hardly eat.

All she could think about was that kiss. She wasn't entirely sure if it could even be called much of a kiss. Elijah's lips had been on hers so briefly that they were gone before she had even realized what he was doing.

It was more so the simple fact that he had done it that she couldn't stop thinking about. As well as the fact that she had *liked* it.

He had obviously been excited about their win, yes. But would he have kissed *anyone*, or just her? That was what she needed to know. But why — *why* did it matter so much?

She trailed her finger through crumbs abandoned by the small sandwich on her plate.

Elijah Kentmore. Not the man that she would ever expect herself to have any sort of feelings for, unless one counted resentment, anger, and, yes, attraction.

But this desire for more, this yearning for him that wouldn't go away — she hated herself for her betrayal. She had vowed to stay far away from him so that he could never hurt her again. Well, now she was opening herself up to the worst kind of hurt possible.

She couldn't let him come any closer.

He might say he had changed, but how could she really be sure? How could she know this wasn't all just some game to him, just like everything else was?

The thought caused her breath to hitch in her throat — could *she* be a game? A bet? The ultimate prank, one she was falling directly into?

She pushed her plate away on the table in front of her as she stood. But when she rounded the small settee, she walked right into the man who wouldn't leave her thoughts.

"Joanna," he murmured, his voice low in her ear, and she wished that he didn't look so dashingly handsome in his black breeches, buff waistcoat, and navy jacket.

"Elijah," she said, attempting to keep her tone emotionless, but when she looked up, he was wearing that I-know-exactly-what-you-are-thinking-about-but-trying-to-deny smile that was both maddening and endearing.

"Ready for a game?" he asked, arching a brow, and she looked up at him quizzically.

"What do you mean?"

He winked at her then held out an elbow, which she took out of politeness — the only reason why, she told herself.

He led her over to a small sitting area in the corner of the drawing room. It was where he had taken up residence the few nights prior when she had first arrived, but today it was full of guests. There was Lord and Lady Oxford, Lord Cristobel, Alex, Caroline, and Cecily and her husband, Lord Danvers.

"Ah, just the people I was looking for," Elijah said as they approached, and Joanna couldn't help but glance up at him again. Just what was he on about? "Who would like to play a game?"

"A game! I would love to!" Cecily exclaimed. "With just us?"

"That was my thought," Elijah said. "The rest might not be interested."

"Shall I ask Baxter?" Caroline asked, but Elijah shook his head.

"He and Ophelia are best with the older set," he said, coaxing a laugh out of the rest of them as he referred to the remainder of the house party, made up of his parents, Cecily's parents, Lord and Lady Hollingtide, and Admiral and Mrs. Cuthbert. "Now, everyone else in? Good."

Joanna could only watch him, mystified. He was such a performer, so at ease speaking in front of the gathered group in front of him. He could command a crowd, hold their attention, make them all follow his every word and action.

She had always been so critical of him for how hurtful he could be that she had never stopped to assess any of his qualities that were actually much more admirable.

"Christmas," he said, lacing his hands behind his back, "is about giving gifts."

"It is not!" Caroline interjected.

"Have you given a gift today, Caro?" he asked, leaning forward and pinning her in his gaze.

"Well, yes, but that's not what—"

"Very well, then. Christmas is about giving gifts."

He looked over at Joanna, tilting his head so that the others couldn't see and winked at her — a gesture she liked to believe was reserved for her alone, although who could know for certain? She narrowed her gaze at his cheekiness.

"What if I told you that I have in my possession the very best gift any of you could have asked for?"

They all looked at him with both curiosity and skepticism.

"What are you on about?" Alex asked his brother.

"This gift is so valuable that I cannot even put a price on it."

"Who's it for?" Alex asked.

"That's just it," Elijah said, unlacing his hands and pointing at the rest of them. "It can be for any of you."

"I don't understand," Cecily said, leaning toward him, her shoulders hunching together so that the tops of her breasts were on perfect display. Joanna would like to think that it was an accident, but she had a feeling there was nothing accidental about it.

"What I am proposing is that we play a game of gift swapping," he said. "We each place on the table a wrapped gift, and then take turns selecting which gift we want. But the key to the game is that when it is your turn, you can either choose a wrapped gift from the table, or you can steal an opened gift from someone else."

They all began talking at once, asking questions or making protestations.

Elijah held up a hand.

"One at a time," he said. "Cecily?"

"The rest of us don't have any gifts prepared," she said, her lips turned down in a pout. "How are we supposed to play?"

"You can choose a prized possession of your own," he said, as though he were offering her a favor.

"What if I don't have anything I want to give away?"

"Well," he said with a shrug. "I suppose you will have to decide if it is worth taking part."

"But we don't know what you have yet!" she protested — quite rightly, Joanna thought, although she would never voice her agreement with Cecily out loud.

"You will just have to trust me," he said, to which Alex snorted, although when Joanna looked at him, he was rubbing his nose as though someone else had done so.

"If we do have something, it isn't wrapped," he added, frowning at his brother.

"Of course you don't," Elijah said. "You knew nothing of my little game until this moment. We shall all take half an hour to go and prepare our gifts, and then we will meet back here."

"I'm not sure..." Alex said, but Elijah just shrugged nonchalantly. "That's fine," he said. "You don't have to take part."

"I think it sounds quite entertaining," Lady Oxford said, and finally the rest of them began agreeing.

"All right," Elijah said, "Half an hour. And remember, do bring something of value to make it fair and interesting. If you don't return, we will know you aren't interested. Away you go!"

Joanna waited beside Elijah until the rest of them had left.

She crossed her arms as she moved her gaze from the bay window showing the snowy field beyond to look at him out of the corner of her eye. "What is this all about?"

"I told you I would get your pocket watch back." He set his jaw determinately. "And I will."

"How are you sure this is going to work?" she asked. "How do you know that Cecily is going to bring the pocket watch? Or that anyone will return to the game? And what, exactly, is this mysterious gift?"

He turned to her, looking around to see that no one was watching before he lightly chucked her on the chin. "So many questions. Not to worry. It will all work out."

"How do you know?"

"Because I know Cecily. She will not want anyone to best her. She will not want it to seem that she owns anything that is less than what the rest of us put out. She cannot help herself from joining in for fear of being left out. As for the others — they will return. Everyone is too intrigued now by what I have to offer as well as how this game will go."

"And this surprise gift that you have?"

"As much as I love standing here and answering all of your questions, that is actually something I must go figure out."

"You didn't even have anything prepared?" Joanna was aghast. "But you lied so effortlessly."

"You should see me play cards," he said with a laugh before beginning to step away.

"There's just one more thing," Joanna said hesitantly.

"Yes?"

She dipped her head, embarrassed to tell him, but unsure what else she was supposed to do.

"I don't have anything to play with."

"What about your new pocket watch?"

Joanna looked up at him, startled, but found only interest in his eyes.

"Well, the thing is…" she said slowly, with a bit of hesitation, unwilling to be vulnerable before him yet unsure what else she could do, "I kind of like it."

The surprise that lit his features was made all the better because it was in no way contrived, and Joanna blushed at the fact that he was now aware that she felt something more for him besides annoyance or anger.

"It is quite a valuable watch," he said, his face masking over once more. "But I'll try to find an extra gift for you."

"Oh, no—" she began, shaking her head, not wanting to ask anything further from him than she already had.

But he was gone, out of the room and on a mission.

A mission for her.

CHAPTER 11

If Elijah wanted to win Joanna's affections, he had to get this right.

He had devised many schemes in the past. Most worked; some did not.

This one had to.

He returned to his bedroom, which reminded him of another man, one who had been quite a schemer in his youth.

Eli wondered how long he would stay here, or whether he might decide to strike out on his own. He still didn't know what he wanted to do with his life. He could return to the army, he supposed, although he had no particular interest in doing so. He could sell his commission or receive half-pay, but what was he to do with his time? Perhaps his father would gift him with a property to manage this Christmas.

He laughed at the thought.

His family didn't trust him. They never had. At least, they hadn't from what he could remember. Elijah scratched his head as he looked around the room with its white walls, green curtains and green canopies. Now that he really considered it, it reminded him something of the forests just beyond the manor.

He rummaged through his bureau, trying to determine just what he could give that would be worthy of the build-up he had noted. He stopped, considering. He could likely give anything he chose; he just had to make them *think* that it was something they desperately needed.

Elijah tapped a finger against his chin as he looked at all that was before him. Finally, he settled upon it.

His souvenir from Portugal. It was a rose that had been dried, crushed between the pages of a large book. That should do it. He gave the rose, instructions to mount it in one of his mother's frames, and the book itself to his valet to wrap before he returned to the drawing room, receiving them back just before the deadline he provided the rest of them.

Joanna was waiting, an eyebrow arched at his return.

"Found something?"

"I did," he said, beaming at her, noticing the way the light brought out the gold hiding within her sleek chestnut strands. He wondered what her hair would feel like running through his fingers. He leaned in close.

"A book from you. A rose from me."

"A *rose?*" she arched an eyebrow, and he nodded.

"All the way from Portugal," he said. "I shall need your help to sell its value."

"What would you like me to do?"

"When you see it, you must pretend that you want it with all of your being — that it would mean more to you than anything else. We need Cecily to desire it badly enough that she will take it over trying to win back her own gift."

"Very well," Joanna said, "although I still—"

"Here we are!" Cecily sang out as she and her husband,

Lord Danvers, approached, their hands full of wrapped packages. "We have our gifts."

She took a sideways glance over at her husband, as though she wasn't pleased with whatever it was he had made her give up. The pocket watch, Elijah could only hope. He was buoyed by the thought that she didn't have anything else with her that she could trade as part of the exchange.

Once they all finally rejoined them, Elijah clapped his hands together.

"Very well, time to begin," he said, grinning at them all. "I can hardly wait until you see what I have. It's unique, it's exotic, and it's from a land far away with quite a story behind it. I've brought a dice as well so we can all roll to see who goes first."

They took turns, and slowly began to unwrap each gift. Lady Oxford went first, seemingly pleased with the book she opened, and Elijah realized he hadn't taken time to review its title. Lord Danvers went next, happy with the bottle of whisky he opened — a good gift, one that Elijah hadn't considered.

Alex then opened the pocket watch, and Elijah's breath caught as he saw both Joanna and Cecily look toward it — Joanna with unquestionable longing, Cecily with a gleam of interest.

Unfortunately, with the roll of the dice, it was Joanna's turn next — he had hoped that she would be able to go after Cecily.

"I—" she looked at him, then back at the watch, "I think I would like the pocket watch."

"You would," Cecily said, but then her mouth quirked at the corner, and Elijah knew why — she was aware that she could steal back whichever gift she chose.

Alex then had the opportunity to choose another gift,

which he did quickly, displaying the pair of cufflinks he unwrapped.

"My turn," Elijah said smartly, then picked what he knew was his gift. He looked around at them all. "I must confess that I am choosing my own gift. I know I shouldn't, but it has to be done."

He unwrapped the package as though greatly anticipating what was within, before delicately picking out the flower that was within a small frame he had filched from his mother's parlor.

Joanna gasped on cue, and he could have kissed her — again — for her excellent performance.

"What is it?" Caroline asked.

"Wouldn't you like to know."

"Well, Eli, you have been teasing it since this game began, so should you not share?"

"Very well," he said, heaving a sigh as though it gave him great pains to do so. "It is a flower."

"That's it?" Alex said wryly. "A flower?"

"Yes," Elijah said with a nod. "And now that I have thought of giving it away... I think I'd like to keep it."

Alex and Caroline, both well-versed in his games, both looked at him skeptically, but he saw he had caught Cecily's attention. She leaned over and whispered in her husband's ear, and Elijah heaved a true sigh of relief that both of them didn't still possess a turn, or else he might have lost it all.

"What kind of flower is it?" Cecily asked, although she leaned back as though trying not to show her interest.

"It is rather exotic," he said, although in truth it was an ordinary rose — one given to him by his nurse who he at first thought had been sweet on him, but, as it turned out, was only pining for her own lost love, to whom he bore a resemblance. "I cannot say that I actually know its name. In Portuguese, it is called a *'rosa vermelha.'*"

"A *rosa vermelha?*" Caroline said, wrinkling her nose. "But that just means—"

"I have heard of those before," Joanna jumped in, "but I cannot say that I have ever had the opportunity to see one in person."

"Well, then, this is your lucky day," he said. "There is quite a story behind it, as well."

"Oh, do tell," Lady Oxford said, clapping her hands together. "I love a good story."

"Very well," he said, settling himself into his seat as he let his imagination roam. "It begins at Christmas — although the Christmas of our story was nothing like the party we currently find ourselves enjoying."

He saw he had their attention now, and he warmed to his tale.

"There was a woman — is there not always a woman? — she was beautiful, of course, with jet-black hair and eyes the shade of violet. Every man who laid eyes on her became smitten, vowing that he would win her affections, but none never did. For her love was held for one man, and one man alone. But he was gone, away at war, and she wondered if he would ever return. She watched for him, waited for him, never stopped looking out the window to see if he might appear. Day after day, the path to her house remained empty, but for the soldiers beyond, marching by as they went to battle, reminding her of his absence in her life.

"Then, that Christmas, as she went to lock the door before going to bed for the night, a shadow on the path caught her eye. He stumbled, but forced himself up the walk and to her door. He didn't even have a chance to knock before she had it open, and went flying into his arms."

He looked up and met Joanna's eyes. Her lips were parted, her green eyes glossy as she waited to hear the end of the story.

"It was her lost love. He had to lean on her to make it into the house, and she led him over to lie down. He looked up at her, his eyes glassy, but was able to lift a hand and stroke her hair back away from her face. 'I love you,' he said."

He paused for a moment, having to fight the lump that had formed in his own throat, knowing how close he had been to becoming this man.

"And then what?" Caroline demanded.

"Then he breathed his last," Elijah said and they all looked at him in dismay. "She kissed his cheek, and as she did, his arm fell to the floor. Within his hand was this flower. She hadn't seen it before. He had picked it for her. She pressed the flower into a book — that book, actually…" he pointed to Lady Oxford's hand, "and saved it. She said that whoever possesses it will always know true love."

"That's beautiful," Joanna breathed, although he noted that his siblings were both still looking at him as though unsure whether or not to believe him — which was fair.

"How do *you* have it?" Lady Oxford asked.

"She nursed me back to health," he said with a small smile of remembrance. "She said I reminded her of him."

"So she gave it to you?" Cecily asked, and he nodded.

"The army was coming. They were going to take over her house and all of her possessions. She wanted me to keep it so that it wasn't lost when they did. She said she would rather someone had it who would take the best of care for it. So here it is. Since you are all so dear and close to me, I know that it would be fine in the hands of any of you.

"Now," he said, breaking the melancholic tension, "I believe it is Cecily's turn."

Cecily looked at the watch, then the flower, then back at the watch again.

Elijah's heart beat rapidly, as it all depended on this

moment, on this decision. He caught Joanna's eyes across the table, and saw the nervous anticipation within them.

"I..." Cecily said, biting her lip, "I think I should like... the flower."

It took everything Elijah had within him not to grin triumphantly.

They continued the game until they were each sitting with a gift, and all relatively happy, he thought — although he couldn't help but notice that Joanna was eyeing the flower with a great deal of interest, and he realized then that she was a romantic at heart.

Dinner was sumptuous, of course, as it always was. His parents were proud of the Christmas feast they put on every year, and this occasion seemed to be no different. He wondered at how there could be a war raging just across the ocean, with so many of England's own taking part, and yet people here continued on as they always had.

He heard Joanna's laughter, and he leaned back in this chair in order to see just what — or who — she was laughing at. Alex. Damnit. His brother wasn't actually interested in her, was he? He leaned back farther, to try to hear what exactly Alex was saying that was so entertaining her.

But then he leaned back a little too far and his chair went crashing to the ground.

Conversation came to a halt all around him, as he looked up to see the holly, ivy, and evergreen pines hanging from high above seemingly staring down at him, laughing at his misfortune.

"Eli?" Caroline and Alex were peering over him. "Are you all right?" his sister asked.

He quirked a smile. "Just fine."

They helped him up, and he tried to grin at the table surrounding him, although his mother, father, and Baxter were all regarding him disapprovingly.

"My apologies," he said with a nod, before waving to the feast spread in front of them, "continue, please."

They were all staring at him with expressions that were a mixture of horror, amusement, and — in Joanna's case — laughter. She was laughing at him. When he met her gaze and crooked an eyebrow at her, she winked at him — a copy of his usual gesture, and he couldn't help but return her mirth.

This had all started as a game, yes, which he was sure she was well aware of. But he enjoyed Joanna Merryton far more than he ever had another.

He only hoped that he had been able to prove it to her sufficiently.

For he was falling for the woman.

CHAPTER 12

It took all evening, but Joanna was finally able to capture Elijah for a moment alone.

Which was crazy in and of itself, as she had been trying to escape him but a few nights ago.

She had to thank him, however, and to ask him if there was any truth to his story. The words had resonated with her, striking her deep in her soul as she wondered if this young woman still loved and what had happened to her.

When he slipped out of the room late that evening as everyone was beginning to retire, she tried to wait a few minutes so as not to be noticed before she quietly excused herself. She caught a glimpse of him retreating into the library, and she followed, quickly surveying the room to ensure that no one else was within.

"Eli?" she called, and he whirled around from the sideboard to face her.

"Joanna," he said with some surprise, "what are you doing here?"

"I wanted to speak to you."

He held his arms out to the side. "Speak away."

She was suddenly shy, hesitant, now that it was just the two of them. While it wasn't the first time they had been alone, it was the first time since she had started to think that perhaps he was not quite so bad as she had initially made him out to be.

Then there was also the fact that she was taken back to the first night she had arrived, when the two of them had found one another in this room. That night, she had wanted nothing to do with him — and had run from his embrace as fast as she could.

Tonight, she wanted nothing *more* than for him to try to kiss her underneath the mistletoe again. This time, she knew she wouldn't push him away. And she most certainly wouldn't try to escape.

She craved his touch, his attention, his temptation.

"I just... I wanted to... thank you for the pocket watch," she said softly, bringing it out of her pocket once more, holding it in the palm of her hand. It fit perfectly. She brought out the other pocket watch, the one he had given her, and allowed it to warm her other hand. "It brings back so many memories. Of my grandmother, of her giving it to me, of Christmases long ago."

She blinked at the suddenly appearing tear forming in her eye.

"Anyway. It means a lot to me."

"Well," he said gruffly, pushing away from the sideboard, "it was my fault that you were without it for so long, so I hardly think that I am the one to thank."

He was right. But even so, she was appreciative of the gesture, as well as the fact that he had gone to such lengths to retrieve it.

"You were quite clever about it all," she said, approaching him, looking up at him shyly.

"Well, that's what I'm good for," he said with a laugh, but

she heard the vulnerability behind it and realized that he didn't think there was much else for which he was.

"You have a skill," she said. "You are quite the storyteller. You can captivate an audience."

"I do my best."

"Tell me," she said, stepping closer still, so that she could look into his eyes, "was any of it true?"

He sighed. "Yes and no."

"What does that mean?"

"There was a young woman who lost her betrothed to war, but he never returned for her. Not at Christmastime or any other time. She did give me the rose, told me I reminded her of her lost love, but it was just a rose from her garden. She was still waiting for him, watching for him, when I left."

"That's so sad," Joanna said, her voice just above a whisper. "I do hope he returns to her."

Elijah was shaking his head. "The letters had stopped, so she assumed the worst. She was probably right."

They were both silent for a moment.

"There is still a lesson in that story."

"Is there?" Elijah looked up, his dark eyes boring into her with such intensity that she nearly shivered. "That war is evil?"

"Yes," she said with a slight nod of her head "That it is. But there is more to it. There is also how important it is to follow one's heart, to take advantage of what you have when you have it, and to not take anything for granted."

"That is... profound," he murmured.

"What was it like?" she asked, knowing the subject lacked romance but unable to keep herself from asking. "Going to war?"

He paused, his hand coming to his drink, still sitting on the sideboard, circling it around the tabletop. "It was... not what I expected," was all he said, and she sighed inwardly. He still had no wish to share with her. She understood, and yet couldn't help but feel some disappointment as well.

"You should get back to the others," he said, turning away from her and walking toward the fire, as though it drew him with its flames, its heat.

"Why?" she asked, unable to help herself from following him.

"You shouldn't be here, alone with me," he said. "You could get caught, compromised. Do you not recall what happened the last time the two of us were alone together? We wouldn't want a repeat of such a thing."

"No?" she said, looking up at him from beneath her lashes. "You wouldn't have any inclination to try again?"

"I know better now," he said, his back still to her, his words a growl, "but I still might not be able to help myself. Not with you. Go, Joanna. Happy Christmas."

She retreated a step or two, looking up as she stopped just underneath the doorway — underneath the mistletoe.

"Elijah," she called softly to him from across the room, "what if I *want* you to help yourself?"

He whirled around to face her. "Did you just say what I think you said?"

"I did."

"You *want* to be caught under the mistletoe?"

"I do."

"By me?"

"By no one else." The words caught in her throat, breathless, wanting, pleading.

He hesitated for a quick moment more before he came striding across the room, stopping just before he reached her. He was an arm's length away and her pulse pounded, her breath coming fast and wild.

She was shocked by his next words.

"I won't kiss you."

"Pardon me?"

"I will not kiss you," he repeated, despite the storm that raged in his eyes as he stared at her. "You have to kiss me this time."

Kiss *him*? She understood why he asked. He had tried to kiss her before, and she had spurned his advances. But she had struggled to find the courage just to step into the library and speak to him, let alone to approach him and *kiss* him. She took a breath. And then another. And then, she looked up into his eyes, so warm and inviting, and his mouth quirked up into a smile, as though he knew exactly what she was thinking.

"What if... what if I asked you to do so for the favor you owe me?"

She wasn't this person — this flirtatious, witty person. Yet somehow, with Elijah, she was.

"You want to waste your favor on my kiss?" he asked, his eyebrows raised.

"Yes, please," she whispered.

He didn't argue any longer.

Before she could close her eyes, he was there, claiming her lips under his.

And she wanted nothing more than to keep him there as long as she could.

For the second their lips touched, all of the fear that had surrounded this kiss rushed away, to be replaced with a wanting so acute it threatened to overwhelm all of her senses.

She was frozen by the thoughts whirring through her mind, of what she was supposed to do now and what he would think of her elementary attempt at returning his expert passion.

But he didn't seem to be thinking anything — for after a moment of him briefly tasting, testing, he seemed to understand that she was welcoming whatever he had to offer, and that tension that had been held simmering beneath the surface finally burst into flames.

With a growl, Elijah closed the distance that remained between their bodies, his arms reaching out and pulling her toward him. Joanna would have liked to have noted that they were no longer beneath the mistletoe, but she was too busy — too busy opening to Elijah as he plundered her mouth like a man who had been desperately searching for her.

His tongue swept inside, and she jumped, unused to the sensation and not knowing entirely what to do, but her body seemed to take over as she simply copied him, parrying each thrust with one of her own. Her hands came around his back, inching up until she twined them into his hair, discovering that his curls did wrap around her fingers as though they belonged there.

He tasted like spicy gingerbread and smooth brandy, and she couldn't get enough.

"Joanna," he murmured, coming up for air, his strong hands with their long fingers coming to each of her cheeks to hold her face before him, "you shouldn't do this to me."

"Why not?"

She could hardly think, so muddled her mind was by the incredible power of his kiss. At least he seemed similarly affected.

"Because it's too hard to let you go."

"I don't want you to."

Disbelief covered his face for a moment, until it broke out into a self-satisfied grin. "Good."

Oh dear. What had she gotten herself into?

He returned his lips to hers, moving his hands to her waist, spanning it with his fingers as he pulled her closer to him in the same motion. Joanna closed her eyes and finally allowed herself to forget all of her misgivings, all of her annoyance, all of her denials against Elijah. Instead, she gave herself over to the sensations he was creating within her, sensations that she never knew could exist.

Joanna could have spent all of Christmas night in the library kissing him, but eventually he left her lips, pressing them against her forehead instead.

"I've never had a Christmas gift so sweet," he whispered against her. "Thank you."

"I believe I enjoyed it just as much," she said, her words coming in a bit of a pant as she struggled to catch her breath.

"Best go to bed now, Joanna Merryton," he said softly, his breath brushing against her ear. "Have yourself a very happy Christmas."

And before she knew what was happening, he had shepherded her out the door and into the corridor, and she had no idea whether she had been chosen or dismissed.

* * *

ELIJAH SHOULD HAVE BEEN PLEASED.

But as he leaned against the closest bookshelf and rested his head upon his hands, he groaned aloud.

For kissing Joanna had only increased his desire for her. He had pushed her out the door before his own passion for her had overwhelmed all else, most importantly his own sense of reason.

He wanted her, yes, but he was well aware that he could not simply make love to her in the library on Christmas night without any sense of commitment — commitment which he wasn't sure he could or should give to her.

For he was well aware there was something still wrong with him, deep inside. His injuries from the war hadn't left any scars. All of his limbs were intact. On the outside, he looked the same man who had left England, though aged by three years.

Inside, however, everything had changed, and the worst of it all was that he wasn't entirely sure just how completely. All of his memories were intact for the most part, but fuzzy. He remembered people, sure. He could recognize friends and family, and had some idea of what he felt about each of them. But particular circumstances, instances, events — they were blurred out, like steam had fogged the glass he was looking through. Little details were difficult to pick up, and he found himself forever trying to make excuses, for he had no idea whether or not anyone could ever understand.

How could one live with a man who might forget his own child's birthday? Who couldn't remember much of his own childhood? Who lived one day to the next, scared that he would forget everything that had come before?

He didn't know what kind of husband that would make him. He hadn't thought he would ever pursue that role for himself.

Until Joanna.

He knocked back the drink he had poured before her arrival, replacing the glass as he left the library to make his way to his bedroom, where he knew he would spend a long, sleepless night, thinking of her, wondering what she was doing, where she was sleeping, if she was thinking of him in turn.

He didn't deserve a woman like her.

But he wasn't sure if he could ever let her go.

CHAPTER 13

With Christmas passed, the Twelfth Night celebration — which rivalled Christmas, and, for the younger set, was likely even more anticipated — was on the lips of all the guests. As everyone gathered in the drawing room several days later, wearing all of the pelisses and cloaks and wool hats and mittens that would be required for sledding that afternoon, they began discussing just what would make for the best celebration.

"Party games are always fun," said Lady Oxford with a smile and a look of knowing at her husband.

"We'll have dinner, of course," Lady Darlington added as she sat and watched the rest of them, for she was staying behind.

"The children can come for a time, can they not?" Elijah asked, and Christopher began bouncing up and down on his toes, while Ophelia rolled her eyes at him.

"Oh, we *must* have a costume party!" Cecily said, joining the conversation. "I *love* dressing up! We can each take on a befitting character. Would that not be fun?"

"I hadn't planned for much by way of costumes," Elijah's

mother said, cocking her head at the thought. "We have nothing prepared. No cards and no costumes."

"The cards are easy enough to make," Cecily pressed. "As for the costumes..." her smile widened, and Elijah suddenly had the feeling that she had an idea which was not going to be in the best interests of someone in the room who wasn't Cecily. "We have a seamstress in our midst!" The expression she sent Joanna's way was one of self-satisfaction for, he was sure, more than just an agreeable thought.

"Oh..." Joanna said with a wince, "I'm not entirely sure—"

"But wouldn't it be fun!" Cecily continued. "It wouldn't be an inordinate amount of work, I'm sure, as we can simply alter the wardrobes we brought with us. Oh, please say you will do it, Miss Merryton, please!"

Elijah frowned. He couldn't say he knew much of the job of a seamstress, but somehow the thought of creating costumes for all of the guests — even if it *was* just altering — seemed to be far too great a task for one person alone, especially one person who was supposed to be here enjoying her Christmas holiday, likely one of the few holidays she ever received.

"I will do my best," Joanna said with a small, forced smile, although she dipped her head quickly, and Elijah just knew that she was hiding an expression of unease at the request. Oh, how he would love to walk over and tell Cecily exactly what he thought, but he wasn't entirely sure where his place was in Joanna's affairs. He was a man who was attracted to her, who had kissed her, who would like to convince her that he was worthy of her affections — but who was also scared. Scared of rejection, that when she learned he no longer possessed all of his faculties, she would run the other way. He wasn't sure which was worse — the man he was before, or the man he had become.

Yet somehow he fervently hoped she accepted him all the same — which was why he had to manage this carefully.

He looked around for Caroline, hoping that she was here to defend her friend, but his sister was nowhere to be found. New worries invaded now as he wondered if she had run off somewhere with the footman.

He knew it wasn't exactly his problem to address, but Baxter was too caught up in his own affairs while his father seemed to have dismissed the thought of Caroline becoming involved in anything more than a flirtation with a footman.

Which was a mistake. For he knew his sister, and once Caroline made up her mind about something, it was nearly impossible to dissuade her. If she thought she was in love with Thatcher, then he knew she would go to any lengths to be with him, even if it was only to prove to them all that she was serious about him.

When he stood to find her, however, he noted that now Joanna was gone as well, and he lifted his hands out to the side and then returned them in exasperation. This house party was going to drive him mad, for more reasons than one.

He turned to find Alex was standing there, drink in hand as he watched him, his expression one of both suspicion and knowing, as though he was well aware just what was bothering him.

"She just left," Alex said dryly. "Cecily arranged for all of the women to bring her their dresses so that she could get to work."

Elijah was already shaking his head. "That isn't right. She's a house guest, not a servant."

Alex shrugged. "She *is* a seamstress. Cecily was right about that. And she agreed." He eyed him with undisguised interest. "Why does it matter so much to you, anyway?"

"It doesn't," Elijah said, masking his concern. It was not

that he cared if his brother knew he was interested in Joanna — as long as she returned his affections. If she didn't, then he had no wish to be embarrassed by unrequited love. Not love, he corrected himself. Interest. "I actually wasn't looking for Joanna — Miss Merryton — anyway. I was wondering where Caroline had gone off to."

"Ah," Alex said, looking around quizzically, "*that* I am not entirely sure about. I haven't seen her in quite some time."

"And that didn't concern you?" Elijah lifted a brow. Why was he the only one who was worried about Caroline? He was supposed to be the one who didn't care about anything but his own actions and how he could entertain all of those around him.

"Caroline is a grown woman," Alex said with a shrug. "If she chooses to ruin herself with the footman, then she must suffer the consequences. She is well aware of what they are."

"And just what would those be?" Elijah questioned. "To marry the man? Father would never agree to it."

"Of course not," Alex scoffed. "No, he would find some other poor sod for her, who would marry her for the family name and her dowry."

"She would hate her life."

"She would. But she would have chosen it."

Elijah heaved a sigh. If he was the only one who had any particular concern about this, then he was the one who was going to have to do something about it. Lord help him.

Or… there *was* someone else who would care. Someone he was fairly sure he could rely on.

She was just rather busy at the moment.

***

Joanna was an excellent seamstress — of that, she was well aware. But even so, she pricked her finger for the second time in a matter of minutes, and she cursed before bringing it to her mouth, sucking on it to stop the bleeding.

Cecily had taken great joy last night in bringing her all of the costumes she was to create, and as Joanna had expected, there was much more work to do than a few simple alternations. Twelfth Night was not far away, but Joanna decided that if she got an early start, then hopefully she could enjoy some evenings before it would be time for the party, and then a speedy return to London. She had been incredibly blessed to be provided with this time away, and she was not pleased with the idea of spending most of it in her room working, but she wasn't sure what else she could have done. To argue with Cecily, the wife of a lord, in front of a room with many other peers would not have been the ideal situation.

She was interrupted by a knock at the door, and she jerked in surprise, stabbing herself again.

"Bloody hell," she shook her head. "Literally."

A chuckle came from the doorway. "Such language."

"Elijah," she greeted him as he let himself in. "Welcoming yourself to my chambers again?"

"It seems I am," he said with a low laugh, one that caused a fluttering in her belly. "There is something I must talk to you about. Two things, actually."

"Very well," she said, holding her hand out in front of her. "Come in."

He did, stepping into the room and shutting the door behind him with a soft click as he looked around him, dismay evident on his face.

"Joanna," he said, his voice softening, "what are you doing?"

"Altering dresses," she said in an isn't-it-obvious way, and he tilted his head as he looked at her while crossing his arms over his chest and leaning backward.

"But why?"

"I was asked to," she said simply.

"You could have said no."

"Could I have though?" she said, looking up at him in supplication from the chair she sat in near the window, where at least she could see out on the day beyond. "I shouldn't even be here," she said with some exasperation. "I may have a trickle of noble blood, true, but I am still a seamstress. I am fortunate to be friends with Caroline. If I wasn't, then the only place I would be welcomed at Briercrest is the servants' entrance."

"That's not true."

"But it is."

They were silent for a moment, and she wondered if this was the first time he had ever truly considered the difference in their stations, and what it might mean.

It was why she was doing all she could to hold herself back from him.

"Cecily gave me a list of all of the costumes," she said, breaking the silence.

"Oh?"

"Do you know what you are to wear?"

"I hadn't given it any particular thought."

"You are the jester," she said, and he pushed himself off the wall at her words, holding himself upright as he studied her.

"Says Cecily?" he ground out.

"Cecily and Ophelia made the list. They are planning the party while your mother is overseeing the food and drinks. Or so I am told."

"I see," he said, his words tense.

"You obviously have no wish to take on such a role," she observed, raising an eyebrow, and he shook his head.

"I most absolutely do not," he said, gritting his teeth. "I've had enough of that throughout my life. I don't need to be placed into the role once more."

"Because you don't like that side of you, or because you think others disrespect it?"

He paused, his eyes locking on hers, as though he had never considered the thought before.

"Both, I suppose."

Joanna looked down as silence reigned again, and she hated that the trust and camaraderie they had built up over the past few days seemed to be breaking as they were both relegated to roles that had not been chosen but assumed and assigned to them.

"Then choose something else," she said, meeting his gaze again. "Choose whichever role you'd like, and I will create the costume for you. Or…" She paused, smiling wickedly, "I can trade you. Let's give Baxter the role of the jester."

Light gleamed in Elijah's eyes.

"He would hate that."

"He would," she said, "but perhaps I just got mixed up. You are much taller than he, but he is much wider. There would be no way to alter the costumes in time once I gave it to him."

"I like the way you think," Elijah said, smiling wider. "Let's do it."

She smiled impishly at him then, enjoying the secret to be shared by the two of them, but then she realized he had said there were two things to address.

"What else did you need from me?"

A kiss… that would do, she thought, the idea surprising her, although she could never be forward enough to say the thought out loud.

"It's about Caroline," he said, sinking into the vanity chair across from where she sat near the window, and he looked out the window, his thumb on his chin. "She and the footman, Thatcher… what do you think of it? Is it just a harmless flirtation, or should I be concerned?"

Joanna bit her lip, unsure of how much she should share.

"It is likely best you ask Caroline."

"I would, if I could find her," he said, "but besides dinner last night, she's been a ghost. What is she doing? You are her closest friend, invited to this house party where you don't know anyone else, and yet she leaves you alone."

"It's not her fault," Joanna said, knowing he was right but unable to help the loyalty to Caroline.

"It is, though," Elijah said. "Please tell me — should I be concerned?"

"I don't think concerned is the right word," Joanna said carefully, her heart unable to resist the despair in his dark eyes. "But I do think that what she feels for Thatcher should not be dismissed lightly. Her feelings for him are strong."

He sighed heavily. "That's what I was afraid of." He began pacing the pink and green Aubusson carpet that lined the room. "I don't even know anything about the man."

"You don't?" Joanna said, surprised. "He's been with your family for years — long before you left for the war."

"He has?" he said, stopping and looking at her, before a mask covered his face. "Of course he has. I knew that."

"Did you though?" she asked, narrowing her eyes at him. "What's wrong, Eli?" she asked softly, and for a moment, she thought that he was going to tell her, to open up to her and reveal whatever it was that had happened to him. But then the moment was gone and his face was shuttered once more.

"Nothing at all," he said with a forced smile. "Just reacquainting myself with my life here. Now," he crossed the room toward her, placing his hands on the arms of her chair, trapping her within it, "come sledding with us."

"I don't know," she said, disappointment invading, for the

thought did sound rather wonderful. "I have so much to do. I really shouldn't."

He rolled his eyes. "And what is going to happen if you don't finish these costumes? Cecily will be upset with you? I honestly don't think that should matter at all."

She considered his words. She did feel an obligation to complete the work, but at the same time... he was right.

"Very well," she said, putting her work to the side. "Let's go."

"That's the spirit," he said, pulling her to her feet and kissing her long and hard, his lips firmly on hers. It lacked the passion of his previous kiss, but held plenty of intention. "We'll have fun — I promise."

His eyes glinted, and she looked up at him, hoping for more but unsure just how to say it.

"What's wrong?" he asked, his eyes searching hers.

"I..." her heart beat hard in her chest, "I'd like, ah, that is —" she swallowed hard. She shouldn't ask. She should leave their relationship as it was, for there was no promise of anything more than a bit of fun, and she didn't trust her heart to leave it at that.

But it didn't seem she had a choice any longer. "Kiss me again?"

"Gladly." He grinned, his eyes lighting in pleased surprise, and then his lips were on hers once more, his hands coming to her back as she placed hers on his chest, slipping her fingers over the top of his waistcoat. Today he tasted like coffee, whisky, and trouble.

Trouble she wanted more of.

Trouble she had always run from.

Trouble she could no longer ignore.

CHAPTER 14

Elijah had spent a great deal of the past few years outdoors.

But battlefields and camps didn't count, he decided as he took a great inhalation of the winter air.

Nothing compared to home, to the grounds of Briercrest, to the scents of pine and snow and fresh crispness.

All made better by the rosy-cheeked woman beside him.

He had finally wrenched himself away from her after their kiss in her bedroom. How he was going to make it through the rest of this Christmastide without taking her to the end of satisfaction, he had no idea. Never had a woman tempted him so, and he wanted nothing more than to convince her that she should be forever promised to him.

The thought should scare him. He had never been one to be particularly concerned with finding a woman and marrying. He had an older brother, who had a son of his own, and before Christopher, if anything had happened to Elijah, there had always been Alex.

But then Joanna had returned to his life, and the thought of marriage was no longer so troubling.

He didn't want to scare her, however, and so he decided he would take things slow. As far as he could tell, she was only just beginning to no longer hate him. That was a good start.

She had donned a pelisse for this sledding adventure, and while he knew the women would likely mostly just watch the children and the men as they slid down the hill, he was looking forward to sharing the day with her.

His sister was here, thank goodness, although Thatcher was accompanying the lot of them as well, dragging the sled behind him. The two of them were practically flaunting their relationship, with their shared glances and inability to look at anyone else save one another. He was of a mind to go tell his sister exactly what he thought, except he knew that it would be met with hostility, and he vowed that today he would bring only fun in order to convince Joanna that she had made the right decision in going along with his plan.

He looked across the snow and winked at her, to which she blushed and turned her head away. He merely laughed and drew near.

"Joanna," he said, nodding at her as though it was the first time they had spoken that day. "Would you fancy a ride?"

Her eyes widened. "A ride?"

"On the sled," he said, nodding his head behind him. "I can pull you if you'd like."

"Oh, no," she said, shaking her head vigorously, "I can walk just fine."

"All right," he said with a shrug. "I would take it, though, if I were you."

She bit her lip but continued to shake her head at him, although this time it was with laughter more than annoyance.

He enjoyed her company as they walked to the hill, the day pleasant and the snow warming into that melty feeling that makes it perfect to create a snowball — although today, he vowed he would not launch anything at Joanna, nor anyone else, in an effort to prove his maturity.

"Come," he said as they reached the bottom of the hill. And a magnificent hill it was.

Evergreens lined the top, so full and so green, but even better, Eli could already smell them from the bottom of the hill, along with the fresh crispness of the winter air. They bordered the hill itself, as though nature had planned this runway with children in mind. The children took hold of the rope of their sleds and began to climb with the energetic enthusiasm that only the very young possess.

Joanna laughed when the first of them came whizzing by with glee, laughter renting the air.

"Let's go down."

"Us? The two of us?"

He laughed. "Yes, of course."

"Oh, I couldn't," she said, her eyes wide.

"Why not?"

"Because, sledding isn't exactly... ladylike, is it?"

He chuckled. "It's Christmas. It's sledding. It's fun. I don't think anyone here will particularly care."

"Perhaps Baxter and Ophelia," she murmured, to which he rolled his eyes and waved a gloved hand.

"No one particularly cares what they think," he said. "Now, race you to the top!"

And with an impish grin he was nearly sprinting up the hill, looking back to see that Joanna had taken his challenge and was charging up after him as fast as she could in the skirts that were swirling around her legs.

He slowed, allowing her to catch up, before sprinting past her to the top, where she joined him, her breath coming in puffs.

"That was not particularly well done," she said, crossing

her arms over her chest as she frowned at him, and he laughed.

"Probably not," he said, as the two of them stood at the top and watched others from their party begin to climb the hill. It seemed that the rest of them were following their lead, as men, women, and children alike were dragging their sleds up. He noticed Lord Cristobel frowning as he watched Thatcher pulling Caroline's sled, and she walked beside him as if the two of them were as paired as he and Joanna — which, he supposed they were. For who were he and Joanna together? They were nothing — yet. But they would be, he promised himself. He just had to do this right. He would court her, win her affections, prove to her that he could be the man she didn't know she needed.

Alex joined them next, one eyebrow raised as he stepped past them silently, and Elijah wondered just what his brother was thinking. He always seemed to be planning, calculating, and sometimes it unnerved him.

Once he was on the other side of them, Elijah pulled his sled forward and sat down on the back of it, before motioning for Joanna to sit in front of him.

"Come with me?" he asked, holding a hand out, and then Alex spoke from beside them.

"You are also welcome to accompany me, Miss Merryton," he said smoothly, "or if you prefer, you can have the sled all to yourself."

Elijah shot him a look of displeasure, which Alex ignored.

"I—" her eyes flicked from one of them to the other, and Elijah wondered if she was truly having difficulty choosing or if she was simply trying not to insult either one of them. "I am sorry, but I had already promised Elijah."

"Very well, then," Alex said with a sigh and then pushed off and was whooshing down the hill as fast as could be.

Joanna stared after him, and then looked to Elijah, who still held his hand out expectantly.

"It's awfully fast," she noted, and he tried not to laugh at the nerves evident on her face as he nodded.

"It is," he agreed. "Come with me anyway?"

She paused for a moment, unsure, but her face then set in determination and she placed her hand in his before stepping forward and settling herself between his outstretched knees. She gripped the front of the sled in both of her hands, and Elijah tried not to make light of her obvious fear.

"You've never been sledding with us before?" he asked.

"No," she shook her head. "I never quite had the courage to try it before." She was silent for a moment. "And there was never anyone willing to take me along."

Her words caused guilty sorrow to fill him, and he hung his head for a moment before lightly touching her shoulder.

"I'm sorry, Joanna. Truly I am. I likely didn't make it any easier on you either. But I am here now. And I promise you that I will make it up to you. Now," he said, placing his hands on either side of her waist, "hold on!"

With a hard push of his heels and hands into the ground, he sent the sled forward. It was an old sled, one fashioned years ago that he remembered using as a child. It was steady and true, sending them flying down the hill. Joanna let out a happy yell of glee and it warmed him through to the core to hear her lose her restraint and allow joy to invade.

The hill was one of legends, steep yet with the perfect slope that allowed for a slowing at the bottom so that one could coast. The footmen had checked the hill to ensure that it was free of debris before the children went down.

Which is why it didn't make any sense whatsoever when suddenly the sled hit a sharp bump, took a quick turn to the right, and they went hurdling sideways, heading for the row of evergreens that bordered the hill.

"Eli!" Joanna yelled out with fear, as he dug his heels into the ground to prevent them from crashing into a tree, even though it sent them flying out of the sled. He wrapped his arms around her and tried to absorb the impact of the ground as they rolled through the wet snow together.

The moment he came to a stop, he was crawling over toward her, checking to ensure that she was all right.

"Joanna?" he asked, rolling her over, and she looked up at him with panicky eyes. "Are you all right?"

"I think so," she said, breathing hard as she sat up, shaking her head from side to side. Her woolen hat was dipped low over one eye, much of her hair falling from its pins to circle her head.

She dusted snow off her pelisse as she seemed to be checking to ensure that she wasn't injured.

"What happened?" she asked, but he could only shake his head in bemusement.

"I have no idea," he said. "We obviously hit something."

He returned to take a look at the hill, one of the footmen, Georges, accompanying him to do so.

"Impossible, my lord," he murmured, shaking his head, "we checked it before anyone went down."

But there, in the middle, almost imperceptibly buried in the snow, was a rock with a mound of snow packed behind it.

It was almost as though it had been placed there on purpose. But how? By who? And why?

He looked around at the others, who began to gather around them, to see what exactly had happened.

Caroline — Thatcher behind her — seemed concerned, of course, as did some of the other guests. Baxter and Ophelia looked slightly annoyed, as though they didn't appreciate the blight on the day. And then Elijah's eye fell on Alexander, who was watching him with what could only be described as a smug, self-satisfied expression. Elijah frowned. His brother would never do something that could so hurt him — was he pleased at the accident after Joanna had dismissed him?

Then Alex looked him in the eye, gave a jaunty wave, and retrieved his sled before going up the hill.

This couldn't be his brother's idea of a worthy prank.

Could it?

* * *

As shaken and embarrassed as she was, Joanna could say with all certainty that Elijah could not have been more attentive following their fall. When she politely refused any further opportunity to go down the hill again, Elijah had insisted that she return home and ensure all was well.

She tried to resist, not wanting to take anyone else away from the fun, but Elijah said that, feeling responsible, he would accompany her. His parents were at home to provide the appropriate chaperoning — not that there was anyone to care whether or not Joanna was chaperoned — and one of the footmen who had accompanied them would follow them home.

Now they had returned, and she was back to feeling unsure. Joanna had never exactly been courted before, and nor had she any idea of whether Elijah was *actually* courting her or not.

He had kissed her, yes, but what exactly did that mean?

"Again, I'm sorry, Joanna," he said, as they stood uncomfortably in the foyer. Her hair hung bedraggled and damp down her back, and she flushed once more as a wet tendril on her neck reminded her of just what she must look like at the moment.

"It wasn't your fault," she said before even thinking on what she was saying.

"It is, though," he countered. "I talked you into coming down with me."

"It's fine," she said. "I'm fine. All is fine."

Did she know any other words besides *fine*? Apparently, it was the only thing she could think of to say.

"Would you like a warm chocolate?" he asked, his hands clasped behind his back, and he looked so eager to make up for their little fall that she felt as though she had to do something to allow him to feel as though he was being useful.

"That sounds lovely," she said. "Why don't I go change and then I will meet you?"

"In the parlor," he said decisively, and he seemed so pleased she had agreed that Joanna couldn't help but feel she had made the right decision.

When she entered the parlor a short time later, however, she found nothing but an empty room. She waited a few minutes, but the fire was in embers and she had the feeling that he had forgotten, or at the very least been distracted. She looked down at her hands, wondering if she was thinking far too much about this and that he, in fact, wasn't particularly excited at all.

He was likely just being polite, she thought with a sigh as she rose and exited the room, beginning down the corridor to return to her own chamber. She had costumes to create. She should continue on and forget that he had asked anything of her.

She was so focused on her new destination, however, that she jumped when a figure appeared in front of her.

"Elijah!" she said, a hand coming to her heart. "You scared me!"

"I did?" he cocked his head to the side. "I've been waiting for you." He waved a hand in the door.

"In the library?" she asked, wrinkling her nose at him. "I had thought we were meeting in the parlor."

"You did?" he asked, raising his brows. "I was most certain it was the library. Oh well," he shrugged, "you're here now. Come in?"

She nodded, slipping past him and into the room. He left the door open as she took a seat in the George III tub chair closest to the fire.

"Where are your parents?" she asked, as he took his own seat in the chair opposite her.

"Upstairs," he said, "likely hiding from the guests for a time. If you feel uncomfortable, I can ask the footman to stay when he brings the tray."

Joanna waved a hand in the air. "There are a few conveniences to being a spinster without any strong noble connections," she said. "One being that no one who particularly cares about your goings on besides as fodder for the latest gossip."

"That doesn't bother you?" he asked as the footman came in with the warm chocolate, and Joanna took a sip, unable to help the gratefulness for it fill her, smiling with satisfaction as she closed her eyes. When she opened them, Elijah was staring at her with a strange look on his face, and she hastily returned to the moment, remembering his question.

She shook her head as she replaced her cup on its saucer.

"No," she said. "Besides, I would not be of any interest to discuss unless I happened to be associated with someone of note."

"Like me?" he asked, raising an eyebrow, to which she nodded.

"Like you."

"Joanna," he began, moving toward her, picking up her hand in his, his skin burning hers, as they had taken off their outdoor gloves and hadn't yet replaced them. "I need to talk to you about something, I—"

But before he could discuss whatever was on his mind —

which Joanna was tense with anticipation as she waited to learn — the door flung open to reveal Caroline at its entrance.

"Joanna," her voice rang across the room, "I have to speak to you."

CHAPTER 15

Joanna was torn.

Torn between concern for her friend and a desperate desire to know just what Elijah was about to say.

She had accepted his offer for a drink together partly in sympathy for him and his apparent guilt over their sledding accident. The other part of her was curious as to whether he had, by chance, anything to do with the cause of it. Had it been some practical joke gone wrong? She didn't want to think such a thing but she couldn't help but be suspicious, knowing his past as well as she did.

And now, the vulnerable emotion on his face surprised her, for he wasn't exactly the type to admit to a feeling of any kind.

Then Caroline had burst in.

Joanna rose, slipped her hand from Elijah's, and walked over to her friend, who she realized guiltily she had somewhat neglected as most of her thoughts had been tied up in Elijah and her time now in the costumes. Caroline, however, had been fairly absent herself.

"Caro," she said, taking her by the hand, "come sit down and tell me what is the matter."

"First," Caroline said with a sideways glance at her brother, "are you all right? By the time I made it down the hill to accompany you home, you were gone."

"I am," she said, reaching for the tray. "Can I pour you a chocolate?"

"Oh, Joanna," Caroline said with a sigh, "I should really be the one doing this for you. I'm so sorry. I have been a beastly friend."

"I was just thinking the same thing of myself!" Joanna responded with a laugh.

They shared a smile of recognition that only true friends could share, before Caroline turned serious once more.

"In truth, though, what happened?" she asked. "We have been throwing ourselves down that hill on those very same sleds for years now and never has one gone so horribly askew."

"I thought the same," Elijah said slowly from his seat. "I think it was tampered with."

"But who would do such a thing?" Joanna asked, and while Elijah shrugged, Caroline's brow furrowed.

"Well, there *is* someone."

"Who?" both Elijah and Joanna asked.

"Oh, Eli, you know very well who."

"I do?"

Now the concern on her face changed from one of suspicion to one rather upset.

"Eli," she said tilting her head, "you've always been quite the prankster, true, but there was never any malice in your intentions. Alex, on the other hand…"

"*Alex* played practical jokes?" Joanna couldn't help but interject.

"Sometimes," Caroline said, "but he usually made it seem

like Eli's fault — especially when someone got hurt. Eli, I'm sorry to say, but you always so admired Alex that you would go along with whatever he suggested."

Elijah frowned, and Joanna wondered just how much he remembered of their youth. It seemed like less every time something came up.

"You think Alex would do something like this, to put me — and Joanna — in danger?"

"Did he know Joanna was going to be with you?"

"He *did* offer me his sled instead," Joanna said thoughtfully.

"My guess is that he wanted to see you look foolish, Elijah," Caroline suggested. "He was the one that was rather sought after until you returned. Now you are not only back, but a war hero at that, and I believe he feels somewhat forgotten. He likely didn't care much one way or the other whether Joanna was hurt along with you."

"That son of a—"

"Careful," Caroline said with a slight smile, "we all have the same mother."

He let out an exhale at that, not completing his prior thought, and Joanna couldn't help but laugh slightly, although with a sigh.

"I will have to get to the bottom of it," he said. "But Caro, was there something else on your mind?"

"Oh," she said, somewhat hesitant now. "I, ah, was hoping to speak to Joanna about it."

Elijah sat back in his chair, his jacket straining over his broad shoulders when he crossed his arms over his chest, and Joanna allowed herself a quick moment to appreciate it.

"I will leave you if you choose," Elijah said, "but I must ask, Caroline, does this have anything to do with the footman?"

"His name is Samuel Thatcher," she said, sitting tall in her chair as though to tell her brother that she didn't appreciate him questioning her feelings toward him. "And you are invited to leave, Eli, if you don't have anything nice to say."

"Caro," he said, leaning forward in his chair, "it is not that I am trying to undermine your feelings or intentions toward him. I just feel as though I need to make sure you understand what it would mean for you to continue this infatuation. If you actually want to be with him, you would have to give up everything for him. Your status, your home, your life as you know it."

"I'm not stupid, Elijah," she said, her face screwed up in consternation. "Do you not think that I am aware of all of this? Furthermore, none of that means anything if I cannot be with the one that I love."

"I know, Caro," he said, his face softening, "I just wanted to make sure."

"Besides," she said, with a quick look in Joanna's direction, "how is what I feel for Samuel any different from what you feel for Joanna?"

Joanna swallowed hard. She and Elijah may have kissed, but they hadn't exactly discussed any *feelings* for one another before, and she didn't think he was about to do so in the presence of his sister.

"That's different," he said, his face hardening.

"How so?" Caroline countered, and Joanna had the sudden urge to leave them and allow brother and sister to talk this out among themselves, but it seemed she was frozen in place, unable to move away from the tableau in front of her.

"Because," he said carefully, as though he was trying to answer her without saying anything regarding his own specific situation, "a woman joins the man's life. It doesn't usually go in the other direction."

"But it could."

"I suppose," he hedged. "But do you think Father would accept a footman joining the family?"

Joanna knew what Elijah was trying to say. Yet at the same time, his thoughts caused an ire to begin simmering in her stomach. Was this how he characterized a person? By their station in life?

"Any more than he would a seamstress?" she couldn't help but say, and both Elijah and Caroline turned to her in surprise.

"Joanna," Elijah said, his tone contrite, "I never meant—"

"I know what you meant," she said, suddenly ashamed for allowing her hurt feelings to take over the conversation, "but still. Something to think about, I suppose."

They were all silent for a moment as they seemed to reflect on all that had previously been known, but somehow, now that it was out there, away from their lips and into the world, it had taken on such more weight.

"Why don't I come with you, help you prepare for dinner?" Joanna asked Caroline, sensing her need to speak to her alone. "Thank you, Elijah, for the chocolate," she said, lifting her cup to him and then taking it with her.

He nodded in return, although his gaze was troubled, his eyes searching, and his melancholy seemed to be catching as Joanna's steps became heavier in turn.

She tore her eyes away and followed Caroline up the stairs, sensing her friend's unease but not understanding the entirety of it until they finally entered her bedchamber and she closed the door behind her.

"Joanna," Caroline whirled around and gripped her hands within her own. "We are leaving. I need a couple of days to prepare, and then we will go in the middle of the night. Or the morning. However you would like to say it — in the wee hours, so that we can make it to Chearsley by first light."

Joanna stood frozen and stared at her friend with wide eyes.

"You and Thatcher?"

"Well, of course, the two of us," she said, her eyes crinkling at the corners as she smiled in excitement. "And you, if you'll come with us."

"Come with?" Joanna bit her lip. "I don't know, Caro, what do you want me there for?"

"To help us," she said a bit desperately. "To be there for me. To convince me that I'm doing the right thing."

Then she sat on the bed, placing her head in her hands before looking up at Joanna in supplication, her smile finally falling slightly as her true worry emerged.

"Oh, Caro," Joanna said, taking a seat next to her. "I cannot tell you what is right with any certainty. Only you know that. What is it that you truly want?"

Caroline sighed. "Ideally, I want to marry Thatcher and live with him in a situation where I can still have a relationship with my family. But you heard Elijah. And he's the most reasonable of them all. I don't see any way forward but to choose — my family, or Thatcher."

"Which brings you the greatest pain to think of losing?" Joanna asked gently.

"Leaving him," Caroline said, her eyes filling with tears. "As much as I don't want to forever say goodbye to my family, they are the ones ultimately forcing me to make this choice."

"Then you know what you have to do," Joanna said. "Where are you going to go?"

"To the village, at least for now," Caroline said. "I'm hoping the vicar will marry us. Once we are married, my wish is that my family will accept us — accept him — but if they don't, we will find a life for ourselves elsewhere."

"What about the banns?" Joanna asked, and Caroline bit her lip.

"I was hoping we could forgo them."

"I don't think that's possible."

"Well, we can always ask," Caroline said with forced brightness. "Now — are you coming?"

* * *

And so, a few days later, in the freezing cold of that time of day that was neither night nor morning, Joanna set out with Caroline and her love toward the village of Chearsley. The snow had melted, but had left an icy sheen on the road, one that they carefully traversed on the sleigh they had borrowed, with Caroline promising that they would return it after they were wed, although Joanna had her own suspicions regarding just what might occur.

She had spent the few days between doing her best to avoid Elijah by hiding in her rooms working tirelessly on the costumes in order to make up for the time she would be spending away. She was almost done — just a few finishing touches to complete, primarily on Elijah's costume, which hadn't seemed quite right as Joanna had worked on it.

When she had seen him, it had been friendly, amiable, but she withheld the desperation for more — for she knew it could never be.

Fortunately, he hadn't visited her alone, for she wasn't sure if she could keep this secret from him, nor how she would respond when he most assuredly would tell her it was a terrible idea.

But this was Caroline's decision, Caroline's adventure — not hers.

When they finally made it to the village church, they were

freezing cold, but Caroline and Thatcher were still infused with a hope that warmed Joanna's heart.

"What's this?" the vicar, Father Franklin, asked when they knocked on the door, and he let them in, still in his nightclothes. "Is all well at Briercrest?"

"It is," Caroline said as he ushered them inside. "It's just... we were hoping that you would marry us."

He looked between the three of them. "Marry—"

"Me and Lady Caroline," Thatcher said, his arm around Caroline in a way that was so endearing it nearly brought a tear to Joanna's eye.

"I know the banns haven't been read," Caroline said, pleading in her voice, "but we would really appreciate it if you would—"

But the vicar was already shaking his head. "I'm sorry, dear, but I can't. You know that. Between the banns having not been read and your family being the most influential in these parts, I could never marry the two of you without their permission. Are you... ah... in the family way?"

Caroline sighed. "It's just that, Father, I know my family wouldn't approve of our marriage, and we really don't want to wait any longer."

"Well," he took a deep breath, "there are a couple of options."

"Which would be?"

"You could try going to Aylesbury, to see what Father McKenzie thinks of the whole thing. He doesn't have to worry quite so much about what your family would think. Or—"

"Yes?" Caroline said hopefully.

"You could always go to Gretna Green."

"Oh," Caroline said, her face falling. "I'm not so sure about that. All the way to Scotland? It would take days, and that is assuming the weather will hold."

"It would," he nodded. "But it is the one sure way to be married."

Caroline and Thatcher exchanged a look, and he gave her a small nod.

"I'm willing if you are, Caro," he said, and the look he gave her was filled with such all-encompassing love that suddenly Joanna knew just exactly why Caroline was willing to sacrifice everything for the man, footman that he was.

Caroline smiled tremulously but bravely back at him, before turning to Joanna.

"What do you think, Jo?" she asked. "Are you willing to continue on with us?"

Joanna hesitated. Caroline had done so much for her that she didn't want to seem ungrateful, but in the same breath she couldn't afford to lose her job, and going to Scotland would basically assure her of the fact.

"I will go with you as far as Aylesbury," she promised. "But if you continue on, then I'm afraid I must stay behind. If I don't return to London by shortly after Twelfth Night, then I will lose my job. They have been generous to give me such time already."

"I understand," Caroline said softly, before reaching out and taking Joanna's hand in hers and briefly giving it a squeeze. "Thank you, Jo, for coming this far with us."

Joanna squeezed her hand back before letting go, and then the three of them said farewell to Father Franklin and returned back out to the cold, to make another attempt at this marriage.

CHAPTER 16

Elijah was troubled but determined.

Troubled, because he knew his words had struck Joanna the wrong way.

Determined, because he was sure that, if he could say the right words, he would make her understand that the two of them could be right together.

But first, there was Caroline. His sister hated him for doubting her relationship, he knew, but if he wasn't concerned for her, then who would be? His parents were never going to approve the union, and how would the daughter of a peer ever learn to work for herself?

At dinner after Caroline's request to speak with Joanna alone, the two of them had been rather silent, speculative, and as much as he tried to draw them each out in conversation, he had ultimately failed. Even Cecily had noticed that something was amiss, and her barbs disguised as enthusiastic praise went unnoticed — except by him.

He was a touch disgusted with his former self. How could he have ever thought himself attracted to such a woman? She was beautiful, true, and he supposed that there hadn't been many options in these parts. But still—

He could tell that Joanna was avoiding him, but what he didn't know was why. He wouldn't push her, however. He wanted her to come to him when she was ready.

A few days later he rose late to find that Joanna had already taken breakfast. He waited for her throughout the day, but she never did come down. When he asked about her whereabouts, Caroline told him that she was working on the Twelfth Night costumes. He was tempted to visit her but recalled her disapproval of his visit last time. Knowing that there was a likely chance he would not be able to keep himself from acting on his attraction once more, he decided against it.

But she never appeared anywhere else — not once, the entire day.

He went to bed cantankerous, determined to wake early the next morning and catch her.

But he was disappointed to find that Joanna was not at breakfast. He asked one of the maids if she had been down, and the girl shook her head and continued on her way. He frowned. He couldn't recall one day since he had returned home that he had been to breakfast before Joanna. But then, he couldn't recall much oftentimes, so he couldn't put much faith in that. But she was used to working, and therefore an early riser. Where was she?

Similarly, Caroline was also not at the table, although his sister was much more likely to sleep late or take breakfast in her room.

As he was studying the table, which was currently only occupied by Alex, Lord and Lady Hollingtide, and Admiral Cuthbert and his wife — whose regard he had been diligently trying to ignore — his attention was caught by a low whispering at the side of the room.

He looked up to see the two footmen who had been serving them had been joined by a passing maid and were furiously whispering to one another, and he was suddenly intrigued by just what had so caught their interest that they would risk the discussion in front of them at breakfast. In his experience, it was the servants who knew more of the goings-on of the entire household than the owners themselves.

Elijah lifted his plate, which was currently nearly full as he had been too preoccupied to eat much, and wandered over to the side table, attempting to listen in to the conversation. He wasn't exactly stealthy, however, and they must have seen him for the whispers stopped altogether.

As the footmen began to return to the kitchen, he caught the eye of the maid — he couldn't remember her name for the life of him — and crooked a finger at her before she could run away. She came slowly, her eyes wide in apparent nervousness. When was the last time he had caused anyone to feel nervous?

"Yes, my lord?" she asked, the pitcher of tea in her hands.

"What were the three of you talking about?" he asked, looking intently at her so that she couldn't flit her gaze away.

"My lord?" she squeaked out. "I'm not sure what you mean."

"Is there something happening that I should know about?"

"I…I'm not entirely sure," she managed, looking from one side to the other as though hoping someone would come and extricate her from this situation, but Elijah was not that generous.

"Tell me," he repeated, more firmly this time, and she dipped her head as she gave in.

"It's Thatcher, the footman," she whispered. "He didn't appear for work this morning. When the butler checked his bed, it was made up but he was gone."

"Gone?" Elijah stared at her, as though by encouraging her to continue he could change the facts of what she said.

"Yes, my lord," she said. "Disappeared."

She bit her lip and looked to the side once more, and Elijah sighed impatiently.

"What else?"

"Well, it is only—"

"Yes?"

"We always knew he had a fondness for Lady Caroline, seeing as he was never interested in any of the rest of us who tried to catch his eye. He's a good-looking one, oh yes he is, and—"

Elijah cleared his throat and gave her a pointed look.

"Right," she said with a nod. "Well, Lady Caroline's maid, Mary, is still downstairs waiting to be summoned by Lady Caroline. She doesn't know if it's her place to say anything, or to go see if she's there, but—"

Elijah took a breath, nodding at the maid as he threw his plate on the side table with a clatter and pushed past her out of the room, knowing that the rest of the table was likely staring after him. He hadn't gotten far when Alex caught up with him.

"Eli, what's going on?"

"Nothing," he said, not knowing why but not wanting his brother to be part of this.

"Elijah."

"It's nothing, Alex," he insisted. "I just have to make sure Caro's all right."

"Caro?" Alex said. "What would be wrong with her?"

"Her maid hasn't been summoned yet," Elijah said as he climbed the stairs, Alex following him.

"So?"

He didn't answer his brother as he continued down the

hall, pushing open the door to Caroline's room without knocking.

"Elijah, what—"

His brother was silenced as they stepped in, finding the room empty, the bedsheets rumpled.

"Elijah, where did she go?" Alex asked finally, crossing his arms over his chest.

"I don't know," Elijah said truthfully, "but I have a feeling she left with the footman."

"Hmm," Alex mused, not looking overly concerned, which bothered Elijah more than the act itself. "Never thought she was actually that serious about the servant."

"Well, it seems she was," Elijah said, rubbing his temples as his head began to ache. "We should have seen this coming."

"What do we do?" Alex asked. "Do we tell Mother and Father? Baxter?"

"What would that do?" Elijah asked. "It would just send them into hysterics and for what? If I'm wrong, it would get Thatcher dismissed before he has the chance to defend himself, and if word got out, it could ruin Caroline."

"That's true," Alex said, and then his eyes lit up and he raised a finger. "I have an idea."

"What's that?"

"It would really throw Baxter over," he said, his lips starting to widen into a grin. "Let's see how long we can make him think that Caroline is still in the house. See how long he can go believing us without actually seeing her. Then once he finally does we tell him that it's been days and this has all occurred because he didn't realize she had actually left Briercrest."

"Alex," Elijah said slowly, "now is not the time for games."

"Oh, come, Eli," Alex said with a wave of his hand. "It is not as though we can change any of this anyway. If this is what Caro chooses, then this is what Caro chooses. Why don't we let her be?"

"Because," he said, not knowing the answer but knowing that he had to make sure his sister was all right. "Because if anything goes wrong, we should be there for her. Because if she really does insist on marrying Thatcher, then she should have someone from her family there supporting her, and we should know just where she has gone to. And because—"

He didn't want to say it. Not to Alex.

But Alex was intelligent enough to guess the truth.

"Because Joanna Merryton is likely with her," Alex said with a knowing smirk.

"Yes," Elijah said, his breath coming out on an exhale.

"I *knew* you cared about her," Alex said, bringing up a finger and pointing it in his face.

"So?"

"So what? Do you think a seamstress is any better than a footman?"

"I don't know Alex!" he burst out. "Maybe marrying a footman isn't the worst of things either. Besides, I thought you were also showing some interest in Joanna."

Alex shrugged. "Perhaps for a flirtation, maybe a fun night or two. Not anything serious."

"She's too good for that."

"Oh, Eli," Alex said with a sigh, shaking his head. "What did the war do to you?"

"Elijah, Alex?"

Baxter and Ophelia stepped out of the chamber down the hall, dressed for the day as they approached. "What's all of the noise for?" Baxter asked, his round face wearing a frown.

"Nothing at all, just a friendly quarrel," Elijah said with a tight smile.

"Well, keep it down," Baxter said gruffly. "We don't want our guests to know about any family quibbles."

Elijah shot Alex a look to tell him that he was right in not wanting to share what had occurred with their brother or their parents.

When Baxter and Ophelia were out of earshot, Elijah leaned closer to Alex and lowered his voice.

"We have to go after them."

"How?" Alex said. "We have no idea where they are."

"No, we don't," Elijah agreed. "But we have to try. You go west while I'll travel east. One of the two villages is their most likely destination."

"Very well," Alex said with a sigh, "although this is not at all how I envisioned spending today. I had a mind to organize a hunt, or, at the very least, sit by the fire with a good brandy."

"Well, life isn't always what we want, Alex," Elijah burst out in frustration, and Alex raised an eyebrow.

"You've changed, Eli," he said, his voice monotone.

"I know."

* * *

WHEN THEY FINALLY REACHED AYLESBURY, Joanna was so cold she didn't think she could properly move. Her toes had frozen into such ice blocks that she bemoaned the thought of how it would feel when the blood began to rush back into them. She could already feel the pain of it. Her fingers had lost their circulation, turning into numb, motionless sticks, while she was shaking so fiercely that her teeth were rat-a-tat drumming their own beat.

Caroline and Thatcher were not immune to the cold, and yet, wrapped in each other, they seemed to be sharing enough body heat to help warm them.

If only Joanna could say the same, but the arms she wished were currently around her were back at Briercrest, likely now growing tense in anger at her departure. At *their* departure. Angry that no one had told him what was happening.

When they entered the small stone church, Joanna couldn't even bring herself to stand in the cold foyer, instead sitting by the fire while Caroline and Thatcher spoke to the vicar.

They were too far away for her to properly see them, but she heard his answer. No banns, no special license, no marriage. At least not here.

The two of them came to join her, dejection on their faces.

"Well, Jo," Caroline said with a brave smile, "this is it, then. We're off to Scotland."

"Are you sure, Caroline?" Joanna said, her teeth finally back under control. "It's freezing out. Scotland is so far. And your family—"

"I'm sure," Caroline said, her jaw set, and Joanna knew then that nothing was going to change her mind.

"Very well," she said, with a warm smile — one she truly did mean — for her friend. "I shall miss you while you are gone, but look forward to your return."

"Me too, Jo," Caroline said softly, "me too."

"We'll take the mail coach to Scotland," Thatcher said. "You can keep the sleigh to return to Briercrest when you are ready. I'm sure one of the men here will return with you."

"Oh, no," Joanna said, shaking her head. "I couldn't. I can find my way back. I—"

"We'd actually prefer it this way," Caroline said. "The stagecoach will be much faster, and warmer for that long of a journey, so you are actually doing us a favor by taking the sleigh home. I wouldn't want to take it from my parents, anyway."

"Very well," Joanna said, resigned, "when are you leaving?"

"First light," Caroline said. "We should all go to the inn, have some dinner and stay the night. We can warm up and hopefully tomorrow brings better weather — for all of us."

"Thank goodness," Joanna said with relief, although she was already thinking about her return to Briercrest — alone — and the fact that she would have to tell all of Caroline's family that she was gone, to be married to Thatcher in Scotland. "Let's go warm up."

CHAPTER 17

By the time Elijah rode into Chearsley, he was bitter. Bitterly cold. Bitterly frustrated. And bitterly desperate to find Joanna.

He had never felt such relief as when Father Franklin told them that Caroline, Thatcher, and Joanna had been to the church and were currently on their way to Aylesbury, but then the vicar had mentioned Gretna Green and Elijah became worried all over again. He could only hope he had made it in time.

When he arrived in Aylesbury, after feeling the fool when he had to ask for directions as he had forgotten just how to get there, he knew he would have no choice but to stay overnight unless he left his horse and hired another. But at this point, he would have to determine just where his next stop was, if one was required, before rushing off to chase them down once more.

He stepped into the inn, weary, cold, and at war over whether his first drink should be whisky or a hot coffee.

Whiskey, he decided, as he secured a room for himself

and asked if the innkeeper had seen three people matching the descriptions he provided.

When the man pointed to the dining room, Elijah didn't know whether to weep in relief or rage in frustration.

Then there they were, Caroline and Thatcher sitting at a table at the far side of the inn, close to the fireplace, huddled together as they ate. They didn't even notice him until he stood right beside them, arms crossed over his chest.

"Elijah!" Caroline finally exclaimed, jumping back and out of her chair. "What are you doing here?"

"What am I doing here?" he repeated dryly. "Caro, what do you think I am doing here? Did you really think you could leave for an entire day and no one would notice?"

He didn't tell her that it was actually Thatcher's disappearance that had first come to everyone's attention.

"Eli," she said, her voice gentling. "I'm sorry. I never meant to leave you all in panic. I truly didn't think anyone would even realize—"

"Where's Joanna?" he asked, unable to allow her to finish, and Caroline's eyes widened. He wondered if he had ever taken such a tone with her before.

"Her whereabouts seem to matter to you," Caroline said instead, her words careful, measured, observant, and Elijah gritted his teeth to keep from speaking out toward her.

"Where is she, Caro?"

"She's upstairs," Caroline said, guilt now crossing over her face. "She has her own room and had to warm up after the journey. She was so cold. I forgot how cold she always gets. I really shouldn't have asked her to come. I—"

But before Caroline could say anything else, Elijah had turned away from her and was beginning to exit the dining room.

"Elijah!" Caroline called out, and he stopped and waited for her response. He would give her a moment, but nothing more. "Before you go, I have to tell you — we are going to Gretna Green. We will be leaving on the stagecoach at first light. It is not up for discussion."

She held herself rigidly, determinedly, with Thatcher at her side, holding her hand in support of her. The look Thatcher bestowed upon her was one filled with such love and admiration that Elijah knew right then that neither he nor anything or anyone else could ever come between them.

He knew something else, too. It was a look that described exactly what he was feeling for another.

"Very well, Caro," he said with a nod. "I only ask that you travel safely, be careful, and when you return to England, be sure to visit."

He surprised her by closing the distance between them, crushing her into an embrace and then shaking a shocked Thatcher's hand. He grinned at them, and then turned and all but sprinted toward the stairs.

* * *

Joanna wondered if she would ever be warm again.

The fire blazed before her as she sat, covered in every threadbare blanket the room had to offer. Unfortunately, her own pelisse and cloak were not exactly made for the harshest weather, and even bundled in it all she shivered. She took a sip of the strong coffee she had requested to be brought up to her room. Caroline had urged her to dine with them, but Joanna could sense that the two of them required time alone, and so she had given it to them. She would return downstairs later on and wish them farewell.

A tear pricked her eye at the thought of her friend leaving. She might be back, true, but she also might not. Caroline and Thatcher could end up anywhere — wherever the two of them might find work and a place to live. Joanna sighed at the thought, hoping that they might consider making London their home.

That idea, at least, cheered her.

She was so lost in her musings that she jumped at the quick rap on the door, trying to hurry toward it but getting caught up in all of the blankets that covered her.

"One moment!" she called out, but then the door opened of its own accord.

In stepped Elijah.

"You should lock your door," he said, standing there in the entrance, looking down at her with some strange expression on his face that she couldn't quite place.

"I wasn't expecting anyone to let themselves in."

"You never know what a man might do."

"No, I suppose I don't."

As they bantered, she was attempting to extricate herself from all of the material enveloping her, but then finally Elijah either noticed or took pity on her — she couldn't be entirely sure which — and crossed over to her.

"Here," he muttered, "let me help you."

Finally she stood unrestricted before him, and his eyes raked over her.

"Why are you wearing your outerwear?" he asked.

"Because," she said with a small shiver, "I'm cold."

"Oh, Joanna," he said, the tension seemingly draining from him as he closed his eyes for a moment. "Thank goodness."

"Thank goodness?"

"I was so worried," he said, rubbing at his temple. "We didn't know where you were. I searched everywhere, trying to find you. I—"

He stopped talking then, crossing to her and then crushing her in his embrace. She closed her eyes and allowed him to hold her, to take away all of the worry, all of the guilt that she herself had been feeling.

"Why didn't you tell me?" he murmured into the crook of her neck. "I would have come. I would have helped. I would have—"

"I'm sorry," she said, breathing in the scent of the winter air mixed with his own masculine musk. "After what you said about Thatcher, I thought you might try to stop Caroline. She was so adamant that no one in her family know until after the marriage occurred, and while I knew I was betraying you, to tell you would betray *her* trust in me. Maybe… maybe if you hadn't seemed so against a marriage to someone below your class, it would have been different."

He tensed at that, and she understood he might be somewhat insulted, but she had to tell him how she felt. And it was the truth.

He stepped back from her, although he kept his hands on her shoulders as he looked deeply into her eyes.

"I know I said that, Joanna. I did. And I'm sorry. I never meant it like that."

She raised an eyebrow.

"Well, maybe I did, but what most concerned me was the thought of Caroline, a woman who has never known hard work, married to a servant of our house. She will face a life unlike anything she has ever known before. I was worried that she wouldn't understand, that she wasn't ready for it. But I was wrong."

Joanna searched his face, trying to determine if he truly meant the words, or if he was just saying them to right his previous wrong.

"Do you know how I know?"

She hoped she did, but she couldn't be sure. She shook her head, just to make him say it.

"I know because of how I feel about *you*. You are far from

a servant, yes, but you were also not raised as part of the *ton*. I find myself, however, not overly caring. It's not a life that I strive toward. I have my own life now, can sell my commission, and I can do with it what I will."

A flicker of hope began to burn in her chest, but she didn't allow it to take flame. Not yet.

"You would go against your family to be with me? As Caroline did?"

He reached out and traced a finger down her cheek, and she couldn't help but nuzzle her chin into his hand.

"I find myself willing to do anything for you," he said softly but intently. "I know I was beastly to you, Joanna, I was. But," he closed his eyes tightly for a moment as he took a breath, and as much as she wanted to hear what he had to say next, she interrupted him.

"Are you all right?"

"Yes. No," he sighed, "just a headache."

She now placed her hands on his shoulders and steered him over to the bed.

"Sit," she said before crossing to the washbasin and rinsing a rag in water. She placed it on his forehead. "Now," she said softly, "tell me what happened to you."

He looked up at her, his brown, full eyes meeting hers, flickering for a moment as the navy ring around them gleamed.

"I'm just frustrated. And a little tired."

She tried not to smile at his attempt to skirt her question.

"You know I don't mean what happened to you today."

He sighed, closing his eyes and lying back on the bed. She lifted a blanket from the floor, wrapping it around her shoulders as she sat down next to him.

"It's not much of a story, really. It was during the battle at Salamanca. I must have taken a blow to the head, but to be honest, I can't remember it actually happening. When I came to, the battle was nearly over, and I was lying there in the middle of the filth and blood and — but you don't need to hear that."

"It's fine."

It did hurt her to hear it, to think of him lying there, all alone, hurt, left for dead. But she needed to hear it. Needed to understand what had led him to becoming the man he was today rather than the boy she had known — or the boy she thought she had known.

"I was a bit confused, unsure of where I was or what I was doing there. Eventually a man from my company found me and led me back. When I couldn't remember what I was doing there or anything much from one day to the next, they sent me to a recovery hospital in Portugal. I slowly improved to the point where they sent me home."

He stopped, looking off toward the dirty window, as though he could see beyond it, back to the battle.

"Why did you go?" she asked softly. She had wondered since Caroline had first told her that his father had purchased a commission. It didn't seem typical of Elijah, and while he had proven himself, she was still curious. Had she so misjudged him?

He looked down at his hands.

"It was actually Alex's idea," he said with a wry smile. "He said it was something we would do together. He told me that I should ask my father to pay for my commission first, said it would warm him to the idea. I thought he was being generous. But then when it was his turn—"

"He reneged," Joanna finished for him, and he nodded.

"He said he wasn't fit for war. I couldn't go back on my request. It was the first time my father had ever actually seemed somewhat proud of me."

Joanna swallowed, compassion filling her for the young

man who had only ever wanted his family's admiration. Who still did.

"Did you tell your family about what happened to you?" she asked gently.

"Not about the memory loss. Just that I had a head injury."

"That's why you didn't remember much when we first… met," she said, unable to help her grin.

He nodded in return. "My memory is getting better — slowly," he said. "I recognize people, but sometimes can't remember their names, for example. I know what I want to say, but sometimes I cannot quite remember the word and its correct meaning. But it's the little things I often forget. When to arrive at places, what I'm supposed to do from one day to the next. Luckily I don't have much responsibility so it doesn't make much difference. Everyone just assumes I'm being my usual self."

"Why don't you tell them?" she asked.

He paused, staring at her.

"It would make me out to be… weak. My brothers… well Baxter is the heir so it doesn't much matter what he does. And Alex… Alex is complicated."

"In what way?"

"He's always been good to me, I think. We are as close as can be. But sometimes I wonder about all the trouble I used to get into, and how much of it was my own doing and how much he orchestrated."

"Why would he do that?"

"For fun, I suppose. A bit of sport."

"Doesn't seem sporting to me," Joanna mumbled, but she began to think on her previous Christmases with the family, remembering instances in which Alex and Elijah had played a practical joke. Elijah was usually behind the scheme, but the intent could be questioned. If Elijah was always trying to do as his older brother wanted him to, then she could see how much of it might not have entirely been Elijah's fault.

"And now?" she asked softly.

He shrugged. "Now I'll likely move somewhere away from the family. Live off my commission or half-pay from the army."

"What will you do?"

He ran his hands over his face.

"I don't know," he shrugged. "I'm not good for much. But I'm also not much of a gambler, nor do I have any interest in the clubs or society events. Unless…"

He had the vulnerability to blush, and it was so endearing that Joanna nearly leaned over and kissed him.

"…I can make it a bit more interesting."

"With a prank or two."

He nodded with some remorse. "Yes," he said.

"So, what would you like to do?" she asked, leaning in. "The world is now open to you."

"Well…" he looked down at his hands, and she realized that whatever it was he refused to say he found somewhat embarrassing, "there is something I would like, but I'm not sure it can ever come to be. Not with the way my mind currently works."

"I don't understand."

Did he want to be a physician or barrister or some such profession? She doubted it, but memory loss would certainly preclude him from those occupations.

He mumbled something so quietly she didn't hear him.

"Pardon me?"

"I said I'd like to be a father."

She sat back, surprised at his words and also… *warmed* by them. A warmth that began in her heart and spread through the rest of her.

"You would make a most excellent father," she said, trying

to hide the emotion that threatened to invade her words. "Christopher and Clementine just love you. Oh, and just think of all the trouble you'll get them into with their mother."

She laughed quietly as a vision filled her mind — a vision of her and Elijah, their children around them. A family.

But. There was a but.

She had to ask.

"Why would you think that could never come true?"

"A man with a condition like mine wouldn't make much of a husband — or a father," he said, his jaw tightening. "Forgetting birthdays, holidays, when to appear, when not to."

"Oh, Eli, I don't think that's anything to be concerned about," she said, tilting her head to the side as she studied him. "Your family — anyone who loved you — would understand."

"But what if..." a pained expression pinched his face, "what if I lose some of the memories that I make with them? What if I don't recall things about my children — things I should know, time spent with them?"

Joanna sat up, coming to kneel in front of him, taking his hands within hers.

"Elijah," she said softly. "No one is perfect. Far from it. But all that matters is that you can prove your love to another. If you have that holding the bonds of your family together, then everything else will fall into place."

His eyes searched hers.

"How are you always so optimistic of what is to come?"

She smiled and shrugged. "It's no use worrying about it. Might as well hope for the best."

He chuckled lowly. "I wish I could be that way."

"I always thought you would be — you're all smiles and laughter and jokes."

"It makes it easier to allow everyone to think that," he

said, and then framed her face in his hands. "I think you're the only one who really sees me for me."

"Because you let me in," she practically whispered. "Thank you."

"No," he said. "Thank *you*. Now." He cleared his throat and stood. "I best get going to bed."

"Very well," she said, although disappointment flared. "Before you go, do you mind stoking the fire? I'd do it myself, but I'm too cold to move."

"Of course," he said, and then walked over and placed the poker in the hearth. Silhouetted by the fireplace, his shoulders were thick, strong, his lower half perfectly framed by his tight breeches.

"Better?" he asked, turning his head over his shoulder, and Joanna nodded, although she couldn't help but pull the blanket tighter around herself.

"Oh, Joanna," he said with a sigh and then sat down next to her. "Come here. I'll see what I can do to warm you up."

She nodded and inched closer toward him, his very proximity sending all kinds of curious tingles up and down her body. He slowly, hesitantly, placed his arms around her, until she was snuggled right up against his chest.

Suddenly she wasn't so cold any longer.

CHAPTER 18

He had told her far too much.
Or, perhaps, it was just enough. For now she was snuggled in to his chest, exactly where he knew she was meant to be. Nothing had ever felt so right before, and a heart beat hard and strong in his ears, although he wasn't sure if it was his or hers or a mixture of the two.

For his blood pumped strong, sure, salacious, just from being near her.

He knew this was a bad idea. Yet when he had finally moved beyond his own memories — or lack thereof — he had realized just how cold she was and knew he couldn't leave her there alone.

So he had done the only thing he could think of — and, to be honest, the only thing he had *wanted* to do since he first saw her underneath the mistletoe in the library — and took her in his arms.

He couldn't see her face, had no idea what she was thinking.

But if the tension he sensed, the longing he felt, was in any way reciprocated by her, he needed to know. For this wasn't close enough. This wasn't cozy enough. It wasn't concupiscent enough. The only thing that would be was her skin upon his, her lips captured in his, her body beneath his.

Not something that one easily told a woman — and he wasn't exactly suave.

"Joanna?" he asked, hearing the huskiness in his voice as he tried to hide just how full he was of need — need for her. "Is this..." he cleared his throat, "is this helping?"

"Somewhat," she whispered. "Perhaps..." she hid her face in his shirt, "perhaps it would be better if we were... closer. Without a layer between us."

She lifted her face up to him now, and he saw the wanting in her eyes that matched his own, along with a vulnerability there, and he realized how much it must have cost her to ask him for this — how much she worried that he might reject her.

She should have no fear of that.

"Are you sure?" he asked, and she nodded, her eyes meeting his, now full of a simmering passion that he hadn't even been aware was lurking there, under the surface. "Skin to skin is the best way to warm one another up," he said, his lips curling at the thought.

"I've heard that before as well," she murmured, and then slowly began to extricate herself from the layers of blankets around her.

He helped her with her pelisse and her outer gown, although he didn't want to completely strip her until he could be there to replace the layers of fabric.

He would do a better job than them at keeping her warm, he vowed, as he removed his jacket, his waistcoat, his shirt.

He pulled her to him then, holding her close as he reached his arms around her and began to unlace her stays, his chin tucked over the back of her shoulder so that he could see what he was doing.

When she was clad only in her chemise, he pulled her forward into the notch between his legs, where she fit just perfectly, and a bead of sweat broke out on his brow as he summoned all of his control to take this slowly. His arms came around behind her, cupping her bottom as he held her close.

"Better?" he murmured in her ear.

"Yes," she said, a hitch in her voice, one that made him smile. She wanted him just as much as he did her. "I don't think I am *quite* warm enough, however."

"No?"

"No," she said, leaning back slightly and lifting her arms overhead. He accepted her invitation, reaching down and finding the hem of her chemise before lifting it overhead. He stopped then, unable to do anything more then to sit back and stare at the woman in front of him.

Joanna, stripped of any clothing, any ornament, any pretense.

"You're beautiful," he breathed, and she smiled hesitantly.

"Thank you," she said tremulously, and as he pulled her toward him, she reached down and began unfastening his breeches, and he thought he might lose his breath altogether.

She seemed expert at it, and for a moment he wondered why until he remembered her profession.

When she had finished her task, she stopped suddenly, as though entirely unsure of what to do next.

That, he could help her with. He stood and shucked his breeches, standing proud before her, and he grinned when her mouth dropped open in shock.

"Is this a joke?" she practically whispered, and he laughed as he shook his head and returned to his knees before her.

"It will be fine," he promised. "I'll make sure of it."

He interlaced his fingers with hers for a moment, before

trailing the tips of them up the inside of her wrist, her forearm, then over her shoulders until he reached her neck. He lifted her hair to the side, trailing kisses over the long expanse of skin, and she moaned so quietly he nearly didn't hear it.

Unable to take it any longer, he wrapped one arm underneath her knees, the other around her shoulders, and then lifted her and lay her gently on the bed beside them. He reached back to the floor for a blanket, then billowed it behind him and lay back above her on the bed, the blanket covering them together, and he dearly hoped that his heat was enough for both of them.

"Are you warming at all, love?" he asked, and her eyes widened at the endearment he hadn't even realized he had used, but she swallowed and nodded.

"I am certainly much warmer than I was before you arrived," she said before her lips curled impishly.

"Let me make you burn," he said, and she nodded, although she seemed slightly nervous, as though she didn't know entirely what to expect.

"Eli?"

"Yes?" He lifted his head from where he was just about to explore her breasts.

"Will you show me what to do?"

His heart nearly stopped at her request. "Absolutely. The first thing you need to do, however, is just relax."

He then began his exploration, beginning with her neck, then down her collarbone to where her breasts began to blossom. He took one nipple in his mouth, first slowly surrounding it with his tongue until he gave it one quick pull. He paid attention to the other before making his way down her stomach.

He skipped over where she was beginning to arch toward him, tracing his hands down her legs instead. His mouth followed, as he kissed every part of her like he would never have this opportunity again.

Except that he now vowed this would not be the last time. She knew the worst of him. She knew what an ass he could be, she knew what faculties he lacked, and still she seemed to want him anyway. He couldn't ask for anything more.

He began to return upward, and suddenly she stilled underneath him when he neared the juncture of her thighs.

"What are you... you're not... that is—"

"Stop thinking, Joanna," he scolded, although without any malice. "Just enjoy."

When he brought his lips to the very center of her, she jerked, her hands in his hair, and he wasn't sure if she was trying to lift him up or keep him there — she likely didn't know herself. He pulled back for a moment, leaving her, testing and teasing her in the same breath.

She didn't seem to appreciate it overly much.

"Where are you going?" she demanded, and he chuckled, returning to his caresses until she was moving against him, and he could tell she was nearing her release. He lifted his head, and she scowled down toward him, making him laugh. She was more temptress than she likely even realized.

He replaced his mouth with his hand, slowly sliding one finger inside of her, loving how ready she was for him and his exploration. She closed her eyes and threw her head back, as he began to thrust in and out as he rubbed his thumb over where his mouth had been.

One hand fisted into the blankets at her side, the other gripped his shoulder, until he felt her begin to pulsate around his finger as she cried out his name. When she had finished, he captured her hips between his hands as he moved between her legs, on top of her.

She was no longer cold, her thighs tight and warm

around him. He was right there, so close, but he needed to make sure this was what she wanted.

"Are you sure?"

"Yes!" she exclaimed, arching her hips to meet his, and he groaned as he could no longer hold himself back from her. He rocked his hips in one last question, holding her green-eyed gaze as he slowly slid into her, both of them silent, captured in wonderment of one another.

Until she winced, and he stilled. He leaned down, kissing her forehead, her temple, her cheekbones, then her lips.

"Relax around me, love."

She nodded, and while she still seemed slightly hesitant, he tested pushing a little bit further. He was barely within, and it was killing him to still and slow, but he didn't want to hurt her, didn't want to scare her.

He already knew, however, that this would be unlike anything he had ever felt before.

Elijah could hear his own breath, intermingled with Joanna's, hard and fast, as his heart pumped vigorously inside his chest. How he had managed to hang on for so long already — through her own climax, through her open wanting of him — he had no idea, but even now, staring down at her, her cheeks hot and flushed, clearly no longer cold, he could just barely manage to keep hold of his control.

She wanted him. She had chosen him. Elijah. A man who had always come second — or third.

He pulled out slightly, then pushed back, a bit deeper. He did so again and again, going a tiny bit farther each time, as he continue to kiss her everywhere he could access — her neck, her shoulder, her cheeks, her lips.

He began to kiss her again, until he finally buried himself inside her as far as he could go, kissing her thoroughly now, drinking in her gasp, as he began to move in time with the love play of his mouth.

He had never known anything so sweet, so perfect, so right.

She was his. Now and forever.

He would make sure of it.

* * *

JOANNA WAS both amazed and in utter disbelief. He was with her. Inside her. Performing the act of love she knew was entirely possible but had never imagined could be so amazing. Astonishing. All-encompassing.

Any pain she had felt began to ebb away as he continued to gently move back and forth within her, and her hands couldn't seem to help themselves as they wandered all over his tight muscles. He was so masculine, so hard, so unyielding, and she wanted all of him, more of him, as his muscles tensed beneath her.

Every time he moved, an exquisite tingle of pleasure traveled up through her, and she looked forward to it with every thrust.

Slowly that same feeling that he had summoned forth but minutes ago — she could hardly believe that it had even happened — began to build once more, a slow burn at first, until it began to steadily increase.

Now she understood why Caroline couldn't keep herself from Thatcher, why she wanted this with him for the rest of her life. It was both absolute pleasure and yet torture in the same breath. She arched upwards, meeting him now, as he began to move faster and faster. His gaze was wild, his jaw clenched tightly, and she could tell that he was doing all he could to maintain control.

He was all she knew, all she wanted, all she never wanted to give up.

She loved him.

She loved this man, who had tormented her, who she had avoided at all costs. Who had moved through war, through pain, to become a better man, one who still held onto that mischievous streak that made him who he was, and yet who now better understood how to keep from hurting another.

But did he — *could* he — love her in return? She had no idea, and it was what kept her from saying it aloud.

He had disdained his sister's attachment to a footman — was this a bit of Christmas fun for him, or did it mean more?

Her heart ached as his heat encompassed her, chasing away any cold that remained. He lifted her legs up from behind the knees to surround his hips and she gasped at how deeply he rocked into her now, their fit so perfect, their rhythm so well timed.

He kissed her again as his thumb found her bud once more and without warning the explosion returned, taking away all of her senses, replacing every thought and every emotion with its intensity. As her body moved against him of its own volition, no longer in time to his movements, he lost his control, banging into her hard, again and again in a frenzy until at last, they both stilled, the only sound remaining their breath, hard and together as they lay there, wrapped in one another's embrace.

"Joanna," he murmured into her neck, where his head was buried. She could but grip him, holding him there, against her, not wanting to let go for fear that this might be the last time she would have him in her arms.

For when they returned to Briercrest — and return they would — what then? With the house as full as it was, she could hardly spend each night in his arms. Then it would be back to London, to the reality that was her life, bent over her needle and thread, creating dresses for other women to wear, women who occupied the same set as Elijah did. Where would he be? What would he do?

She didn't know, but didn't want to ask for fear of shattering the moment.

The pace of their breathing finally slowing, he rolled to the side, pulling her in close to him, her chest against his as one strong arm came about her possessively.

Her body was on fire now, and she could hardly imagine how she could have been as cold as she was just moments ago.

She tried to enjoy the moment — truly she did. But her thoughts were wild, and she couldn't help but ask, "What do we do now?"

"Now?" he asked, then looked at her mischievously, his brown eyes glinting.

"Now we sleep for a while. Then we wake up and do it again."

"Again?" she squeaked.

He nodded. "It seems to me that our greatest gift this Christmas is this time together alone." He chuckled. "And we have Caroline to thank for it, it would seem. Now," he said and kissed her forehead, "get some sleep. I'll keep you warm."

Her questions could wait until the morning, Joanna finally realized. This felt too right. Too peaceful. She snuggled her chin into his chest and fell fast asleep.

CHAPTER 19

Elijah inched out of the bed the next morning, standing and stretching his arms and legs, bending over to unkink his back.

It was not the world's most comfortable bed, but he had no care whatsoever for how it felt — it had served its purpose and provided him the best night of his life.

He located his clothes, tossed around the bed and the floor, and he dressed as quietly as he could so as not to wake Joanna. She looked so beautiful, so peaceful lying there, her hair fanned behind her on the pillow, one hand out on the bed beside her, where it had previously been upon his chest.

He would have dearly liked to remain with her, but he had missed dinner the previous evening and was starving, and he knew she likely would be too. He wanted nothing more than to have breakfast with her, but they could hardly go together downstairs. He would descend himself, ask for a tray of food, then return with it. He would be gone but a few short minutes, and was sure that she would still be sleeping when he returned.

He slipped out and down the stairs to find that the dining

room was nearly full, but rather subdued. He sat down at a table and lifted a hand when he saw the innkeeper look his way.

The man ambled over to him, asking him how he could help him. As Elijah began to request a simple breakfast and some pastries, the man's wife walked up to him, whispering lowly in his ear. The innkeeper frowned, ignoring Elijah, who finally leaned forward and held up a hand.

"What's the matter?"

"You haven't heard?" the innkeeper said, looking up at him in surprise.

"No," Elijah said impatiently. "I just came downstairs — how would I have heard anything of note?"

"Of course," the innkeeper muttered. "There's been an accident just outside of town early this morning. The stagecoach overturned. My wife tells me now that it seems a few people were injured."

Elijah's heart stopped. "The stagecoach?"

"Yes," the innkeeper said. "It was near empty, but from what I'm told there is concern regarding a young woman. We just heard of it. They are all still there."

Elijah didn't stop to hear anymore. All he could think of was that his sister was on that coach. He pushed back his chair, grateful that he had brought his cloak with him. He threw it over his shoulders and was nearing the door when it burst open, and a bedraggled, nearly crazed Thatcher stumbled in.

"Thatcher!" Elijah gasped, taking him by the shoulders and shaking him, likely much harder than was due. "What happened? Where's Caroline?"

"She's in the carriage still," he said, his eyes looking around him wildly. "We need a physician. I didn't know where to find one, so I came here. It's the only building I knew. We stayed the night, then left early this morning. Knew you were here..."

He didn't seem to have any control of his emotions nor his words, and Elijah realized that he had likely been so shocked from the incident that he had lost any sense.

"Will you come? Will you help me?" he asked, his focus finding Elijah once more. "There are people there, but—"

"Of course," Elijah said with a firm nod. "Of course."

He looked back, finding the entire dining room was staring at them.

"Find the physician!" he shouted to the innkeeper, and then followed Thatcher out the door. "Let's go," he said as they stepped out into the snow, only to find a familiar figure coming up the path.

"Alex!" he called out to his brother, who approached, looking as weary as Elijah himself had felt yesterday. "Did you hear what happened?"

"About the stagecoach?" he asked with a shrug. "What of it?"

"Caroline is in it," he said, "we're going to her now."

Alex finally seemed to register Thatcher's presence. "I'm coming," he said, immediately returning back the way he had come, but he looked so cold that Elijah knew he would be no help whatsoever.

"Go warm up. I'll go with Thatcher," he said, nodding toward the inn as a niggling thought invaded the back of his mind. He was forgetting something, but what?

Suddenly a flood of memories came rushing back from the night before, along with a sense of guilt over having completely forgotten.

"Joanna," he said, surprising both his brother and Thatcher. "Joanna is still at the inn. Sleeping."

Alex's eyebrows raised as though he wondered just how

Elijah was aware of what she was currently doing, but he didn't remark upon it.

"Stay there," Elijah said with a wave of his hand. "Warm up in the dining room. When Joanna comes down, tell her what happened. I'll be back shortly. Can you do that?"

Alex nodded. "Of course. Go make sure Caroline is all right."

Elijah looked back, finding that Thatcher was already nearing the stable. He understood his urgency. If it had been Joanna who is in trouble, he would be wild with worry.

"I'll be back."

* * *

JOANNA WOKE UP LANGUIDLY, stretching her arms over her head. She was sore, and yet... strangely satisfied. Why? What had happ—oh. Oh, yes.

She remembered now. She opened her eyes and rolled to her side, reaching out, expecting to find Elijah, her lips already curling into a grin at the thought.

Her hand came up empty.

She opened her eyes, finding nothing there but the impression of where his body had been. She sat up, holding the blanket around herself as she looked around the room.

No Elijah. Nor any sign that he had ever been here.

She frowned as she swung her legs over the side of the bed. She supposed that this is what she should have expected. He had likely been thinking that they should avoid being found together, that was all.

Perhaps he was downstairs.

She dressed as well as she could without any help. Her blasted stays were too difficult to do alone, so she ended up just managing to tie the ends, but so loosely they nearly fell off when she pulled on her dress.

A knock came at the door and she ran over to it, opening it hurriedly, convinced Elijah was on the other side.

She was to be disappointed.

It was a middle-aged woman she supposed was the innkeeper's wife.

"Pardon me, my lady, but I noticed you were without a maid and I was wondering if you needed any help getting dressed."

"Actually, that would be lovely," Joanna said, stepping back and turning around so that the woman could quickly help her with the last of the fastenings.

"Will there be anything else?"

"No, thank you," Joanna said, not wanting her to linger, for she was eager to go downstairs and find Elijah, who was sure to be in the dining room having breakfast. Perhaps he was waiting at a table for the two of them, she reasoned.

When she descended the staircase, she looked around the room, searching out his dark head of hair, that silhouette that she would know anywhere.

But he was nowhere to be found.

Instead, another familiar figure stood from one of the tables and approached.

"Joanna."

"Alexander," she said in surprise, "what are you doing here?"

"Won't you have a seat?" he asked, ignoring her question as he swept his hand out to the chair across from him, ignoring her question.

She dutifully sat, but she wouldn't let him free from his question, which she repeated.

"I was looking for you."

"For me?"

"Well, you and Caroline and Thatcher," he expanded. "The three of you gave us quite the merry chase."

"Yes, that is what Elijah said, and I do apologize to you, as I did to him."

She paused for a moment, hoping she wasn't revealing too much when she asked, "Have you seen Elijah?"

He ignored her again, aggravating her further, instead continuing to tell her how he had come to find her.

"Elijah traveled east; I went west to Oakley, but, finding no sign of you anywhere, I circled back, arriving here. I had an inkling this is where Caroline would be, anyway. As it turns out, I was right."

"She left," Joanna said simply, accepting the cup of tea the innkeeper poured her with a thank you.

"I'm aware," Alex said, waiting to continue until the innkeeper had left them. "Took the stagecoach, I'm told."

"Yes," she inclined her head. "I was to take the sleigh home with the horses. I just need to hire someone to drive me. Caroline left me money to do so, but I suppose if you and Elijah are here now—"

"Ah, yes, Elijah," Alex said, his lips turning into a smile she recognized, one that she had always thought was a laughing one, particularly at Elijah's pranks, but now it gave her something of an icy shiver. Was there more to this smile of Alex's than she had originally thought? For if she wasn't mistaken, he seemed rather... satisfied. Smug. "I actually had breakfast with him this morning."

"Did you?" she asked, looking at the table in front of her as though there would be evidence of his meal left behind, but all she saw was Alex's own cup of coffee.

"I did," he said, and then chuckled. "You slept in. You had a late night, I hear."

Joanna's cheeks burned hot, angry with embarrassment. "Elijah told you?" She knew the brothers had once been close, but she had never thought he would betray her like that.

"Of course he did," Alex said, leaning back as he leveled his gaze upon her. "He had to."

"Why would that be?" she asked, even as a voice inside her head was shouting at her to stop asking questions and find Elijah herself.

"So that he could collect his earnings."

"His earnings?" she echoed, although she was no longer able to fully follow what he was saying. Her body suddenly felt awkward, cold, as though she was not completely inside of it but hovering just above it, half in and half out.

"Oh, my dear Joanna," he said, his smile falling as he tilted his head and looked upon her with pity. "You didn't know. But of course you didn't."

"Know what?"

"Well, you know how Elijah is."

She did know how he was, but she wasn't sure if she and Alex were reflecting on the same aspects of his character.

"Yes…"

"When you joined the house party, so soon after his return, I told him it must be fate. He laughed at that, although he agreed that you could easily fall for him. We made a bet on it. I thought for sure I would win. After all, you were not keen on his affections whatsoever at the start and I knew how much you hated him from years past. But then, however he convinced you, he did it well, for by the end, you were quite enamored with him. Caroline's little scheme played perfectly into his hands, for it apparently afforded him the opportunity to bed you as he wished."

Joanna could only stare at him in shock and utter horror.

"You're lying," she finally managed, although she heard the own lack of conviction in her near-whispered words.

"Why would I lie about such a thing?"

Her thoughts returned to last night, to Elijah's tender words, to the way he had made love to her, to the promises he had sealed with his words and with his actions. Although... he had never said anything about what the future would hold — for him, or for the two of them.

"He just... he wouldn't lie about it," she said, but the words and the excuses were flimsy, even to her ears.

"Oh, Joanna, you poor thing," he said, and Joanna wished she could reach out and smack that look of pity off of his face. "You believed the best in him. But Elijah is Elijah, and he will never change."

"He did," she insisted, shaking her head, still unable to believe Alex's words, despite the drips of doubt that began to invade, "he did change. The war changed him."

"One can never truly, completely change," Alex argued. "I'm sorry, Joanna, but look at the facts. Where is he now? You would think that after a night together, he would be here awaiting you, but instead you find *me* at your breakfast table. He left — went home. Didn't want to have to face you, wasn't man enough to tell you that none of it meant anything."

But it had meant something. It had meant *everything*.

She closed her eyes, trying to keep the tears from falling as she fought for breath, despite inhaling deeply unable, it seemed, to get enough.

"Why are you still here?" she finally managed, proud of herself for keeping the tears at bay.

"I hadn't finished my breakfast, so I told him that I would wait for you and tell you that he had pressing matters that took him away. But I decided that you deserved to know the truth."

"Well... thank you," she said, although she didn't mean anything of the sort. Every inch of her had gone numb. Everything she had imagined, all that she had envisioned for the two of them vanished in but moments.

For as much as she hated to admit it, there was one glaringly obvious fact that she couldn't ignore. If Elijah cared anything for her, he never would have left.

"I... I have to go," she said, pushing back and away from the table abruptly, the tea left half-finished in front of her, but she didn't think she could manage another sip.

"How are you going to get back to Briercrest?" he asked, and she just shook her head, unable to even consider it. She just needed to get out, away from here, away from the place where she had thought her life was beginning but where, in fact, it was all being taken away.

"I'll escort you home."

"No!" she practically shouted before calming herself. "No thank you. I would like to be alone."

"I'll hire a driver to escort you home," he said, much more kind than Alex had ever been before. Why was he doing this for her? Did he feel guilty for his brother's actions? "You can take my horse."

Joanna had no idea what he would need the sleigh for, but she supposed she wasn't in any position to question it or to argue.

"Fine, thank you," she managed instead.

Joanna wanted nothing more than to say no, to get away from the entire family — except Caroline, but she was well away from here — but she didn't have much choice. She still had belongings back at Briercrest, for she had only packed for one night away.

She would return, collect her things, and then take the next stagecoach for London. It was all she could do.

For she had been well and truly tricked, and she was the greater fool for having allowed it all to happen.

She should have known better.

She *had* known better, but she had allowed her heart to overcome what her mind already knew.

And she would never allow it to do so again.

CHAPTER 20

*E*lijah had felt relief many times before — at the end of a battle, when he determined that his friends were still alive, when he found himself in one piece.

But he had never felt relief quite like this.

For now he was returning not to a lonely tent where everyone was melancholy and morose — a circumstance not much better than the battle itself.

He wasn't even returning home, but that didn't matter. For it wasn't that he was returning somewhere, but rather to some*one*.

He closed his eyes, able to picture each moment of his night with Joanna as vividly as it had occurred, which was both a miracle and a mercy. He could hardly wait to do it all again.

Caroline was, blessedly, all right. She had taken quite a tumble in the carriage, but despite Thatcher's insistence that she be thoroughly checked over by a physician, she was declared well and healthy — just bruised and scratched.

And cold. They were all cold.

He was hardly off his horse — Caroline and Thatcher

traveling in the physician's carriage behind him — when he was passing the lead off to the stablemaster and nearly running through the door and into the inn.

He came to a stop when he found his brother, alone, sitting in the dining room, lazily twirling one ankle where his leg was crossed over the other.

"Elijah," he said with a nod, "how is everyone?"

"Caroline is fine," he replied. "Thatcher is seeing to her." He looked around the room. "Where is Joanna?"

"Oh, Joanna," Alex said with a sigh, standing and walking to the door, where Elijah stood, still clad in all of his outerwear. "Unfortunately, she is gone."

"Gone?" Elijah said, looking at his brother incredulously. "What do you mean, gone?"

"I mean just that," Alex said with a shrug as though it were of no consequence. "When she learned that you had left her, she decided that you were not worth waiting for. Something about, once a jester, always a jester."

"She did not say that."

"Perhaps not in those words," Alex said, waving a hand in front of him. "But she is looking for a *man*, Eli. One who can care for her, provide for her. You can hardly take care of yourself."

"I would disagree, for I did through three years of war," he said, gritting his teeth, his spine stiff and straight with suspicion. He had a feeling he knew just what had run Joanna off, and he didn't think it was her own assumptions.

But what caused this pang deep in his chest was the question of why she would have believed anything but the truth. Why had she not believed in *him*, and in what he felt for her?

Because he had never told her any of it, he realized. They had been so busy enjoying one another that they had never stopped and shared with one another how they actually felt.

He had been scared of rejection and he supposed she had felt the same.

And now she was gone. He hoped returning to Briercrest and not all the way to London, for if she had, he had no idea how he would ever find her.

"How long ago did she leave?" he demanded to Alex, who shrugged lazily.

"Shortly after you departed."

"That was hours ago!" Elijah exclaimed, aghast.

"So it was." Alex sighed. "She's likely returned to Briercrest by now."

"What did you tell her, Alex?" Elijah pressed, angry now.

"It's just a joke, Eli," Alex said with a bit of a chuckle, but it was no laughing matter to Elijah.

"Did she seem to find it humorous, Alex?"

"Do any of the people we are pranking, Eli?"

Elijah rubbed his temples where the headache had formed long ago but was now pounding in earnest.

"No," he said, shaking it, "but we were wrong. And that was years ago."

"What about the prank on Baxter?" Alex asked.

"Well..." Elijah bit his lip, "I suppose old habits can be hard to break sometimes. But I'm doing my best. That, however, is not something I need to prove to *you*. I'm going, Alex. I need to find Joanna."

He stopped, turning suddenly toward his brother. "Why didn't you accompany her back?"

"She was quite clear that she had no wish to be in my presence — nor yours," Alex said.

"Where did she go?" Elijah asked quietly.

"Wouldn't you like to know."

Much to the surprise of most of the patrons, Elijah suddenly lost his temper. He rushed forward, taking Alex by the collar, pushing him back up against the wall.

"Where. Is. She?"

"All right, all right," Alex said, holding his hands up. "She went back to Briercrest. She said something about collecting her belongings."

Elijah pulled out his pocket watch, reminding him of Joanna and her own.

"If I leave now I can hopefully catch her," he said before casting a reproachful gaze upon his brother. "Let's just hope there is enough time."

* * *

Joanna stared at the costumes that currently lined her bed, mocking her, waiting for her to continue.

They were nearly done. All but one — the one that mattered the most.

She hadn't wanted to make Elijah's costume into the jester, but perhaps it was appropriate, she now considered.

He would have to figure out how to finish it himself. For she was done. She was done with it all.

She opened the wardrobe and ripped out the few dresses she had brought with her, stuffing them, along with the rest of her meagre belongings, into her valise.

At least, out of all of this, Caroline had found her happy ending. She had discovered enough love for both of them.

Joanna had snuck in through the servants' entrance, and they had been respectful enough of her to promise to keep her secret. She figured they considered her as much one of them as she was one of the guests she had dined with each night.

She just needed to get out of here without anyone knowing she had arrived. That way she could avoid any questions about her absence, as well as that of Caroline's.

She took one final look around the room, and opened the door to leave.

Only to find that there was no way out.

The entrance was filled with a man, tall, broad, dark, and angry.

Joanna hated the fact that underneath the anguish his presence caused her was a deep yearning for him all over again.

One of his hands now came up against the top of the doorjamb as he stared down at her.

"E-Elijah," she stammered, feeling rather lost for words. "Wh-what are you doing here?"

He lifted his brows.

"What am I doing here? Well, first off, I live here. Secondly, I'm here to keep you from leaving."

Her jaw dropped. "Keep me from leaving? I think that opportunity passed this morning, when I woke up alone and found that you had not only bedded me and left me, but that it was all to win some stupid bet against your brother."

She was not normally one to be overcome by anger, but now she was fueled by hurt at his absence. "How could you do such a thing?" she said, near tears.

"Joanna..." he held his hands up as he stepped into the room and shut the door behind him. "Calm yourself and listen."

"Calm myself?" she repeated, narrowing her eyes at him. "You cannot be serious?"

"I understand you're angry, but I am too," he insisted. "How could you believe such a thing about me?"

"How? I will tell you how. You are the same man who made me kiss a dog in front of all of your friends. Who caused me to lose a pocket watch that meant more than I could ever properly explain. Who placed coal in my stocking.

Who says he is changed but just the other day pranked his brother into making a fool of himself."

Elijah hung his head, scratched his temple, dug his toe into the carpet, before finally looking up at her.

"You're right. I am all of those things. But…"

"But what?"

"I want to be more. I want to be better. You make me want to be that way."

"Well, I don't seem to be doing a very good job of it, for as far as I can see, nothing has changed. You make fun at other people's expense, and then think that an apology can make everything better. Well, that won't work with me, Elijah. Not anymore. You are not the man that I thought you were, that I thought you could be. I promised my grandmother when she passed that I would never settle, that I would live the life I wanted, that I would find the most happiness that I could ask for. I thought…" her voice caught, but she swallowed the sob and carried on, "I thought that could be with you, but I was wrong. Now, please move. Let me leave. Let me go back to my life — the life that may not be the Christmas fairy tale to be found here at Briercrest, but is a life that I made for myself and that I deserve. Can you do that? Please?"

He didn't move for a moment. His head lifted and his eyes caught hers, and for a moment what she saw was such pain, pleading, and supplication that she nearly apologized, gave in, and told him that she had been wrong and that she would choose her desperate longing for him over her own happiness.

But she remembered her grandmother, remembered her words of always choosing what would bring happiness. And she held strong.

"Very well," he said quietly, "if that is what you want."

She could only nod.

He dipped his head, stepped to the side, and she picked up her bag and ran out of his life forever.

* * *

JOANNA COULD HARDLY BREATHE. She was running away from the house, down the path to the stables, knowing she would have to rely on the benevolence of one of the grooms to take her as far as the next town, where she could catch a mail coach and return to London, far away from Briercrest and all of the promises and memories it held within it.

She had no idea how she had managed to keep herself together when she confronted Elijah, but now out here, in the icy coldness of the day, the tears began to flow, hot and wet, so at odds with the crispness in the air.

She was so blinded by her tears that she didn't even see what was in front of her until she heard a voice cut through her despair.

"Joanna? Joanna! What's wrong?"

"C-Caroline?" she managed, stumbling into the stables, blinking rapidly in time to see Caroline and Thatcher, standing next to one of the horse stalls. "What are you doing here? What's going on? What?"

"After everything that happened, Elijah convinced us to come home," Caroline said, exchanging a look with Thatcher. "After he left us, he told us he was going to collect you at the inn, ride home with you, and then would meet us here in the stables after he had a chance to talk to our parents, to try to soften them for our return. We traveled home with Alex in the sleigh."

"I don't understand. What do you mean, after everything that happened?" Joanna demanded, suddenly so confused and wondering if she had been tricked again. It seemed she could no longer separate truth from fiction. "When did you see Elijah?"

"You don't know?" Caroline asked, her eyes widening, and Joanna shook her head fiercely.

"But I thought you had returned to Briercrest — that you and Eli rode home together. That's what Alex told us after we made it to the inn. Eli had been at the carriage."

"We had an accident," Thatcher said gruffly, pushing off from the post he had been leaning against. "Caroline was injured."

Joanna gasped, her eyes running over her friend. "Oh, Caroline, are you all right? How did it happen? What did you hurt? Why—"

"I'm fine," Caroline said, before she and Thatcher told the story of how the mail coach had hit some ice and overturned. Caroline had been knocked around, and Thatcher had been overly concerned, calling for the physician.

"But what did you injure?" Joanna asked, curious as to how her friend could have been so gravely hurt and yet was now standing here before her.

"I..." Caroline and Thatcher exchanged a look before Caroline leaned in to her, lowering her voice, "I'm expecting."

"What?" Joanna practically shouted, and Caroline lifted a finger to her lips.

"Please, Jo, keep it a secret?" she pleaded. "We would prefer that no one was aware until after we were married, for we don't want anyone to think that this is *why* we are marrying."

"Of course," Joanna said, but then stepped toward her and wrapped her arms around Caroline. "Congratulations. I'm so happy for you. And I assume the baby is fine, then?"

"As far as we know," Caroline said with a small smile, and Joanna took a deep breath. "But Joanna, how did you not know about it? When Thatcher found Elijah at the inn, Eli rushed to help, but said that Alex remained, and that he would explain all to you. When we returned to the inn, you and Eli were both gone. Alex said you had ridden back to Briercrest together."

A thick curl of apprehension began to snake through Joanna's stomach.

"I—… did see Alex," she said, her voice almost a whisper, "but he didn't tell me any of that."

"What did he say?" Caroline demanded, her eyes narrowing.

"He said…" Joanna swallowed. Caroline was her best friend in the world. They didn't keep secrets from one another, and yet Elijah and Alex were her brothers. "Alex said that my time with Elijah was the result of a bet that the two of them had made. That Elijah cared nothing for me and that this was just another of his pranks. Oh Caroline…" she said, a hand coming to her forehead as realization washed over her in a wave, "what have I done?"

"What *did* you do?"

"I saw Elijah… told him that I could never be with him, that he wasn't the man I had thought he was, that he hadn't changed and I could never be happy with the likes of him. Pushed right past him and out the door. And he… he let me go."

"Oh dear," Caroline said, biting her lip. "It was all a great misunderstanding."

"Yes," Joanna said, but hesitated, "except that I could have chosen to believe in him. To trust in who he was over what Alex tried to make me believe."

"It's not your fault—" Caroline began, but Joanna was already shaking her head.

"It *is* my fault, though, Caro," she said, and then looked up at her friend in supplication. "What should I do?"

"What do you *want* to do?" Caroline asked her frankly.

"I want…" A horse whinnied from the stall over, as though encouraging her, and Joanna took a breath. "I want to be with Elijah, truly I do. But I have no idea if he feels for me as I do for him. And he let me go so easily…" she paused, hesitating, and Caroline reached over and placed her hands on Joanna's shoulders.

"I have never, in my life, seen Elijah as happy as he is when he is with you. I think, Joanna, that you have to take a chance. Hope for a little Christmas magic. Put your trust in Elijah and what he feels for you, in who the two of you can be together. Trust me," she looked back at Thatcher, "it's worth it."

"You're right," she said, a glimmer of hope beginning to form and flicker. "I will try."

She looked up at Caroline. "I have an idea," she said, "but it will take some time. Will you promise not to share that I am here?"

"You are going to stay then?" Caroline said hopefully.

"For a time, at least." Joanna nodded. "I have to make things right. And I want to be here for you if you need me."

"Very well," Caroline said, her brown eyes serious. "I don't know if anything will have changed," she said with a deep breath. "But Elijah has convinced us to try."

Joanna squeezed her hands. "I must go before Elijah comes back for you. I will be in my room if you need me. Please tell me how everything goes with your family. Once they know how in love you are… I hope they will understand."

"Me too," Caroline said fervently. "Me too."

CHAPTER 21

While he hadn't had any wish to face his family at the moment, Elijah had promised Caroline that he would do what he could. And while he wanted nothing more than to hide away in his rooms and drown himself in his misery, he had promised his sister. If he could see one happy outcome from today, then perhaps he could convince himself there was still some vestige of hope for love in this world.

It had nearly crushed him when he had heard Joanna's words, when he saw that while she had been deeply hurt, it was because she had no belief in him whatsoever.

He had let her go when he realized that he would never be good enough for her, that he could never overcome the shadow of his past that he carried around.

He had almost forgotten his promise to his sister after his conversation with Joanna, but a glance out the window, the stables in his view, reminded him of their plan. If he couldn't have Joanna, he would make sure his sister's Christmas wish came true. He had spoken to his father, and while he didn't have any promises, there was an inkling of hope.

He ducked into the stables to find Caroline and Thatcher.

"Took you long enough," she called out to him as he walked in. "We're quite close to freezing in here."

"Oh, it's warm and you know it," he countered. "Besides, it's time for you to come in, anyway."

Caroline looked at him with consternation.

"He said no, didn't he?" she asked, her face falling, and she reached behind her and took Thatcher's hand in hers. "We're leaving, then, Eli. Come, Samuel, let's go before—"

"No, Caro, wait," Elijah said, holding out a hand. "That's not it at all. Father does want to talk to you, and I think it's a good thing."

"Really?" she said, lifting a brow beneath her wool cap. "Then why are you looking as though we've lost the war?"

Because he had lost Joanna, the best thing that had ever happened to him.

"Nothing to do with you," he said with a quick shake of his head. "Come."

He hoped for his sister that the reunion between her and his parents would be a joyful one, but as it happened, he didn't have the opportunity to witness their reaction, for his father asked for a moment alone with Caroline. Both Elijah and Thatcher attempted to accompany her, but she turned to them, shaking her head.

"Thank you both, but I shall be fine," she said with a small, brave smile before stepping into his office.

Elijah and Thatcher shared a look, before Elijah tilted his head to the side, then motioned for Thatcher to follow him into the parlor that shared a wall with his father's study.

This room wasn't often used, and despite the fact that it had been opened up for this house party, a musty odor lingered, one that even a good cleaning couldn't quite remove.

Eli lifted a finger to his lips, then led Thatcher over to the side wall, collecting two hardback chairs on the way. He pointed up toward the ceiling, to where the transom window overtop of the door was slightly ajar.

They took a seat, and sure enough, soon his father's voice came through the window at the top.

"Caroline," he said, his voice gruff from years of smoke curling around his throat, "I am very disappointed in you."

There was a pause.

"I understand, Father, but *you* must understand something as well. I love Samuel Thatcher, and I am going to be with him, despite what you think. I know he is a footman, but he is a good man — the best man I have ever known. I love him, and—"

"Caroline," her father's voice was softer now, "that is not why I am disappointed. It saddens me that you would think that to be the case."

"Then what—"

"I am disappointed that you would run away from the family. Especially during Christmastide. We had no idea where you were, if you were safe, or what had become of you. If Elijah hadn't realized that Miss Merryton had gone with you, we would have been most frightened. I—" his voice broke, and Elijah started. He hadn't been aware that his father possessed such depth of emotion. "I was worried I had lost you forever."

"Oh, Father," Caroline said, and Elijah could picture the two of them embracing.

He snuck a look at Thatcher, who was running a hand through his hair, his eyes wide and incredulous. Elijah didn't blame him.

"Now," Eli's father said, obviously sufficiently recovered, "if you are sure you want to marry Thatcher—"

"Oh, I am, Father, I am."

"—then we had best start making some arrangements."

Elijah could only sit there, his eyes wide as he listened to it all.

He had been so hurt by Joanna's inability to believe in him that he had forgotten one thing — how much he loved her. How much he hoped she loved him.

He had to put his hurt feelings aside and understand that past misdeeds could cause great present misunderstandings. But things could change, people could change, and they needed to work through this — together.

If Caroline and a footman could have a future, then surely so could he and Joanna?

"I have to go," he whispered to Thatcher, who nodded and stood, following him out of the parlor.

He reached out his hand, and when Thatcher took it, he pumped his arm up and down a few times. If the war had taught Elijah anything, it was that a man was not made by his station. Thatcher seemed a good enough sort, and if he was Caroline's choice, then he would welcome him as a brother-in-law.

"Best of luck," he said, and then turned to go.

"Same to you," Thatcher called after him, and when Elijah looked back, he caught his knowing grin.

He would pack his bag, and then he would go find Joanna. He couldn't let her go again.

* * *

JOANNA HAD NEVER sewn so fast or furiously in her life. Thank goodness all of the other costumes were ready. It was just Elijah's she had to perfect.

She found Caroline's maid, Mary, who was astonished to find Joanna within the house. She had many questions, of course, but Joanna just shook her head as she told her that she would reveal all later.

"Right now, we need to get these costumes to where they need to go," she said, and Mary nodded, although Joanna could tell that she was fighting her curiosity.

Arms loaded, Mary continued to carry the costumes, delivering them to the appropriate rooms. On her last visit to Joanna's room, she took in her hands the one remaining costume.

"For Lord Elijah," she said, and the girl held it out in front of her, staring at it,

"It's perfect for him," she said with a surprised glance at Joanna and Joanna smiled softly.

"It is, isn't it?"

If only he would understand just what she thought of him, and how she loved the man he truly was.

* * *

Elijah had no idea what to pack. What did one take with him to London to chase down the woman he loved?

Warm clothes, he decided, looking out the window as he stuffed another greatcoat in his bag.

There was a knock at the door and he called out for whoever was there to enter. He was surprised to find a maid standing in the doorway.

"Lord Elijah?"

She held in her hand a bundle of fabric, and he couldn't help but tilt his head to try to determine just what it was that she held.

"Yes?" he said, impatient to get on with it. He would prefer to catch Joanna sooner rather than later. One never knew what the weather held.

"I have something for you, my lord, a costume."

"I won't be here for the Twelfth Night celebration," he

muttered, trying not to rush the maid out the door but wanting to nevertheless. "It can go to someone else."

"She said it was for you specifically."

"Who said that?"

"Miss Merryton, my lord," the maid said, and when he took a closer look at her, he realized the girl's eyes were practically shining.

"When did you see her?" he demanded, and the girl shrank back from him ever so slightly.

"Ah… just a few moments ago?"

Joanna. She's still here. "Did she say anything else?"

"Just that she looked forward to seeing you in it this evening."

"Thank you," he said, taking the garment from her, suddenly needing to see it immediately. He unfurled it, allowing it to lie down across the bed. It stared up at him as though it had life within it. He swallowed hard.

It was the costume of Joe Giber, the king's jester, as had always been planned, he could tell, but it wasn't the typical costume. There was more to it… the sparkling gold along the edges, the crown, the red cape as though he was the king himself. The jester… and the king, together? It made no sense. Unless… unless she was trying to send a message.

Elijah stood there for a moment, stunned, unsure, but then he flew into motion as fast as he could.

He called out for his valet, hoping the man would come speedily. He was there shortly, and the good, steady fellow didn't comment on Elijah's absence nor the valise packed on the floor, nor the costume he immediately wished to wear.

He had no idea what time the festivities would begin, for he hadn't been planning on attending. He no longer cared, however, for Joanna would be there, waiting for him. He sincerely hoped she would be wearing the costume of the queen she was, the queen he knew her to be despite what she might otherwise think.

He wondered what it meant that she hadn't left. Had she determined that whatever was between them was greater than his faults?

The fact that this costume was both jester and king told him that she understood that some aspects about him were never going to change... but that she accepted him for it anyway.

Or so he hoped.

* * *

"Joanna?"

"Caroline!"

Joanna drew her friend into the room and enveloped her in an embrace. "Did you speak to your father?"

"I did." Caroline's face was radiant. "Oh, Joanna, you might never believe it, but he has actually accepted the fact that I will wed Thatcher and has even given us his blessing. We are to be married once the banns are well and properly read."

Joanna warmed all the way through in happiness for her friend.

"I'm so glad, Caro," she said. "What changed his mind?"

"You know," Caroline said slowly, "I think it just might have been Elijah. It's hard to even think of it, but since my father spoke to him, it seems that he changed his mind about a lot of things, really."

Joanna had to blink back tears. She had been so wrong about Elijah, in every way possible.

"Have you seen him yet?" Caroline asked, and Joanna shook her head.

"I haven't," she said softly. "I only hope that he can find it in his heart to forgive me."

"Of course he will," Caroline said confidently. "If you could forgive him for all that he did to you years ago, then I'm sure he can do the same."

"He's a different man now," Joanna murmured, "even if he hasn't shared exactly why."

She turned around, nerves filling her as the dress on the bed stared back at her. Could she do it? She, a seamstress, don such a creation?

"It's beautiful," Caroline said, following her over and staring down at the garment.

"But should I wear it, is the question," Joanna murmured, and Caroline placed a hand on her shoulder.

"You most assuredly should," she said confidently. "Besides, you've already given Elijah his costume. Who else is going to match him?"

"But what about the others? They might think—"

"It doesn't matter a fig what they think," Caroline said, crossing her arms over her chest and leaning back against the bedpost. "I am marrying a footman. I'm sure they will all have plenty to say about that. But you know what, Jo? I don't care. For what matters is that I love him, and I am going to be happy with him. Even if I have to become a housemaid myself."

"You're right," Joanna said softly, hope beginning to fill her. "Anything is possible."

"That's the spirit," Caroline said. "Now, let's get this costume on you so that you can become the woman you were meant to be."

"Should we call for the maid?"

"No, I shall help you," Caroline said, and when Joanna was about to argue, she held up a hand. "It shall be good practice," she said with a laugh, and, resigned, Joanna turned around and lifted her arms.

CHAPTER 22

There was no party quite like Twelfth Night.
Especially Twelfth Night at Briercrest.
It had been a few years since Elijah had been home for his parents' end-of-the-Christmas-season party, but it seemed nothing had changed. If anything, the revelers were in much higher spirits than ever.

There were the usual guests from the entirety of the Christmas house party, of course, but this was the one night each year when all societal classes no longer seemed to exist, when everyone was in costume and was someone else — or some*thing* else — for the evening. Villagers and servants alike were in attendance, and it had always been Elijah's favorite evening of the year.

Some revelers wore masks, while others wore elaborate costumes, many, he knew, sewn by Joanna's hand.

Never again, if he had anything to do about it. The only costumes she would be sewing would be those for their children, he vowed.

That thought alone caused a fierce yearning to race through him.

He dimly noted telling his mother that she looked beautiful, while his father passed by in his servants' costume and told him that he would like a moment to talk to him in his study later. Elijah nodded absently, a small part of him curious about just what his father would like to speak with him about — likely something to do with Caroline and Thatcher — but not overly caring at the moment.

There was but one thing he cared about right now. And that was Joanna.

Where was she? Even if she was obscured by a mask, he would not only know her form, but would be able to sense her presence.

And then, suddenly, he did. So did everyone else in the room. Cecily and her husband were speaking to him — although about what, he had no idea for he wasn't even listening — and Cecily stopped mid-sentence and stared up with a gasp.

For there, at the top of the staircase that led from the upper entrance down to the ballroom, was Joanna.

Perhaps others in the room weren't aware that it was she, but he knew.

He could tell by the way she moved, by the way she carried herself, by the small, steady, unsure step she took as she began to descend the staircase.

He didn't do it consciously, but he felt himself moving toward her, drawn by her, needing to be close to her side.

He met her when she reached the bottom step, holding up a hand to her as he bowed low.

"Your Highness," he said in a hushed voice, holding out his hand, as a crowd began to form around them. The odd whisper invaded his ears.

"Who is that?"

"Why is she dressed as the queen?"

"Oh, what a dress."

But none of the whispers mattered.

The only voice he needed to hear was Joanna's.

He led her onto the dance floor just as the musicians struck up a waltz. He glanced over toward them to find that his sister had been directing them, and she smiled broadly at him.

He tugged on Joanna's hand, pulling her toward the floor. She resisted for a moment.

"Elijah, I have to tell you—"

"Shh," he said, "one dance, first."

"But—"

"One dance?" he asked this time, and she finally nodded, allowing him to lead her.

He grasped one of her hands, tightening his other around her waist, so grateful, at the moment, to simply have her in his arms once more. How could he have ever thought he could give her up, no matter that he had assumed he was doing so for the right reasons?

Elijah knew people were watching them, but he was glad of it. They should all see Joanna for who she truly was, for how she deserved to be regarded.

"You are beautiful," he said, hearing the awe in his voice, needing her to know of it.

She blushed most becomingly.

"It's the dress," she said, looking down at herself. "It was the dress I wore on Christmas, but I made a few... modifications." She leaned in close. "To be honest with you, I used a fair bit of fabric that Cecily provided me to make hers."

"Your secret is safe with me," Elijah said with a laugh, and she smiled up at him. "But it's not the dress. You could wear anything and be simply stunning."

"You look quite handsome yourself," she said.

"Why, thank you," he returned, "although in my case, it most certainly is the costume that has made the man."

The song came to a close, and he bowed low over her hand. He noticed a figure coming up behind her, and he was well aware that many would be requesting her name for a dance.

"Come," he said, tugging at her hand once more, "the jester has a trick to play — I am going to make you disappear."

"Disappear?" she echoed, following along with him.

"Just for a time," he said, as he led her through the corridor, past doorways that had previously been filled with mistletoe and other greenery — all which had been removed and were now burning in a roaring fire in the drawing room.

"Where are we going?" she asked breathlessly.

"You'll see," he said, leading her down before finally stopping just before the library. "Joanna—"

"No," she said, holding out a hand and shaking her head, "I must speak first."

"Very well," he said, rather liking the command in her tone.

"Elijah, I'm so sorry," she said, hanging her head slightly, but he reached out and lifted her chin so that he could look into her eyes. "I didn't believe in you, and that was wrong. I should have known that you would never leave me, that this would never be some great joke to you. I had thought that, perhaps, the boy you used to be might have done such a thing, but the man you are now never would. You would never hurt me like that.

"The truth is, Elijah..." her voice caught for a moment, tears filling her eyes, "the truth is that I love you. I love you so much that it hurts. I know that I am but a seamstress, and likely not a woman you would ever have seen yourself with, but I needed you to know how I feel. And I need you to know that you are more than worthy of finding a woman who will believe in you just as thoroughly."

"Oh, Joanna," he said, reaching out and brushing away a tear that was traveling down her face with his thumb, "you have nothing to be sorry for. I did you wrong many years ago, it's true. Yes, we can blame Alex, but I was just as much a part of it. Even when I first saw you here in this library at the beginning of this Christmas season, I wanted you because of your beauty, not taking time to find the woman you were beneath it all. But over this Christmastide, I have been blessed, because I have been provided the opportunity to know you, all of you, and I am a better man for it. That you would ever doubt me is my own fault. But—"

Why did there have to be a but?

"Yes?"

"I don't know... that is, my mind isn't what it once was. There is an excellent chance that I will forget things that are important. That I won't remember your birthday, or the servants' names, or maybe even our own wedding."

She only smiled at him, her lips curling softly.

"Then how fortunate I will be there to remind you of it all."

He nodded at her and then turned around, backing up through the doorway, coming to a stop just on the other side.

He crouched down on one knee.

"Joanna, there is one thing I promise to never forget — and that is how much I love you," he said reverently, holding out his hand. "I have but one Christmas wish, and that is this — will you become my wife?"

She stood there for a moment, saying nothing, and his heart nearly stopped as he waited, praying that she would agree.

"Oh, Eli," she said, tears beginning in earnest now, "of course I will."

He stood then, taking her around the waist and bringing her in close to him. He bent his head, touching his forehead to hers, the crowns they both wore clashing against one another, causing her to giggle.

"I have a secret of my own," he whispered.

"Oh?"

"Before the festivities began, I made sure that the mistletoe remained above this doorway."

"Oh, Eli," she said pretending to hit him in admonishment, "you could be inviting the gremlins that way, leaving greenery up past Twelfth Night!"

He laughed, long and loud, in gaiety that he had been missing for a long time now.

"I'm willing to risk it," he said, "but if you're that concerned, I promise to take it down, after first putting it to good use," and then he leaned down and took her lips in his, no longer able to hold himself back.

Oh, how good she tasted, he realized as he moved his lips over hers, licking the seam of them until she opened to him and he swept his tongue inside, exploring, plundering, promising a lifetime and more.

She clutched his shoulders as she returned his kiss with equal measure, and he ran his hands down her back, pressing her in against him, so that they were as flush as could be between the layers of clothing that separated them.

Clothing that suddenly seemed to be far too cumbersome, too numerous between the two of them.

But first, he sunk his fingers into her hair, tilting her head so that his mouth just brushed the soft skin between her ear and her jaw. He nibbled, tasted, then feasted as he she hummed her approval.

His other hand lifted, his thumb brushing over her plush lips, and she opened them slightly and allowed it in before sliding it back and forth from one corner of her lips to the other.

He trailed his mouth down her neck to her collarbone

from where it began at her shoulder to where it ended at her throat. When she moaned, he lifted his hand to follow the path his mouth had traveled, until he reached the top of her bodice and finally slipped his hand beneath it, shoving aside the stays and chemise until he found what he was looking for.

The hunger in Joanna's eyes mirrored his, and he released her hair, needing to rid her of this infernal costume — although he did appreciate that it highlighted the queen she truly was.

"Joanna," he murmured, "my queen, no matter what you are wearing."

And with that, he went to work on the hooks and eyes, longing to rip them down the middle, but knowing how hard she had worked on this costume — on all of the costumes.

Beads of sweat broke out on his brow from his concentration on removing each tiny, infernal fastening that he suddenly felt she had sewn just to tantalize him. She laughed lowly, apparently sensing his dismay, as she moved against him, and then, finally, he decided enough of this, and he pushed the bodice down as far as he could until her breasts were free.

It would do — for now.

* * *

Joanna had been tempted to help him.

But, as agonizing as the wait was, it had also been all too amusing to watch Elijah's struggle with the back of her dress.

And then his patience had worn out.

Finally, when her breasts were free, he sat back on his heels and stared at her, blinking.

"You are so beautiful," he murmured, looking up at her, his eyes dark with need.

She cupped his chin in her hands. "You're not so bad yourself," she said with a laugh, reaching down to untie the top of his breeches on the costume that she had fashioned herself.

Swallowing any nerves, she congratulated herself on her bravery as they fell away, and he stepped out of them, shucking them to the side as she swallowed at the sight of him. She had seen all of him before — had *felt* all of him before — but somehow it was still a shock, to think that this beautiful man before her was hers, that he wanted her, that he thought her as attractive as he apparently did.

"I love you, Joanna," he said, stepping close to her, catching her against him. "I love everything about you."

He lifted her skirts high and then gripped her hips beneath them, so his bare fingers were upon her. In one powerful motion, he had her lifted up and on top of the sofa at their backs.

Joanna didn't think he could move quickly enough, and she threw back her head with a moan when they joined together. Suddenly all of their words of love and tender caresses were forgotten, as the moment turned into one that was devoted to their need for one another.

Elijah set a quick pace, one which led Joanna to loop her arms around his neck and hold on tightly, as the intensity he took her with soon sent her flying to her peak, fire exploding within her belly and spreading through her limbs with an unimaginable force. Elijah buried his face in her neck and groaned as he clung to her in desperation.

For a moment, Joanna lost herself and became one with him, completely bound to him as they declared themselves to one another.

Finally, slowly, consciousness returned as Joanna became aware of Elijah, softly crooning in her ear. She leaned back and took his face within her hands, cupping his chin as she searched his eyes, finding only peace.

Elijah slowly smiled, his eyes dark and soul searching as he sighed in satisfaction.

Joanna ran her fingertips up and down his back, and he shivered at her touch.

"I love you too, Elijah," she said, finally answering him, and he laughed lowly as he leaned in and took her lips softly and quickly.

"Now," he said, "are you ready to return, as queen of Twelfth Night?"

She laughed lowly, kissing him once more.

"Only if you're my king."

"Always."

CHAPTER 23

*J*oanna had been somewhat worried about their return to the ballroom, as though everyone would know simply by looking at them where they had been and what they had been up to.

But she had nothing to be concerned about. During the time they had been gone, it seemed that everyone had truly lost all of their inhibitions, and the party was in full merriment.

House guests, servants, and villagers alike were now in the midst of a truly scandalous, merry dance as they all filled the ballroom floor.

The only attention she and Elijah received as they entered was from Caroline, who greeted them with an excited kiss on the cheek for both of them and then pulled them into the middle of the melee.

They danced long enough that they were both ready for a drink themselves after a time, and Elijah pulled her to the side and began to murmur in her ear as he nuzzled it in the same breath.

Joanna nearly swooned once more, until she opened her eyes to find a figure just beyond Elijah's shoulder.

"Eli," she murmured, "Alexander is here."

He growled low in his throat before turning around to see his brother as well, although it seemed that Alexander had not yet seen the two of them.

"I know that I am supposed to be a changed man," Elijah said to Joanna, "but what do you say about a little mischief this Twelfth Night?"

"I say that sometimes a little mischief is called for," she said with a wicked smile, and he laughed.

"What do you have in mind?" she asked, and then he proceeded to explain his plan. By the time he was done, she laughed in anticipation. "I love it," she said, then did as he bid and made herself scarce, hiding at the side of the room, behind one of the columns where she could watch the proceedings.

Elijah walked over to his brother, his shoulders stooped as he played the part of a jilted lover. Alexander reached out and clasped his shoulder, to which Joanna rolled her eyes. Surely he didn't think that Elijah wouldn't have found out about his attempt to keep the two of them apart?

She saw Alexander's head rise and a satisfied smile spread across his cheeks as Elijah shared with him the fib they had discussed — that Joanna had chosen Alexander and was awaiting him.

Elijah left him, then, and walked over to the column Joanna was hiding behind.

"Let's go," he whispered, and then they raced out of the room and down the hall so that they could arrive before Alexander did.

They took their places in the shadows of the room, where they would be hidden from view, but present — they wanted to play a joke, yes, but not actually cause any harm to come to Alexander or the person he would be clandestinely meeting.

The door eased open, and first Cecily entered the room, a bounce in her step as she took a seat on the sofa and spread her skirts out around her. She fluttered her hands around her hair, checking that it was perfectly in place, and Joanna had to bite back a laugh at how she was primping for her apparent rendezvous with Elijah.

She leaned back on the couch, spreading her arms behind her as though to showcase all that she had to offer.

With a creak, the door again opened, and Alexander stepped in, rubbing his hands together as though he was getting ready to sample a tasty treat — which, Joanna supposed he was.

"Cecily!" he exclaimed, coming to a halt when he saw her spread out before him. "What are you doing in here?"

"I…" she began, pausing as she did so, "I thought that… that is, I… oh dear," she said with a sigh. "I was waiting to meet another."

"As was I," Alexander said, narrowing his eyes as he seemed to understand just what had happened, although Cecily was still oblivious. "Were you meeting your husband?" he asked, and Cecily's mouth opened and shut a few times like a fish.

"Yes," she said decisively with a nod, "that is what I was doing. And you?"

"Looking for my brother," he said.

Elijah shifted, making a bit of a scuffle that caused Alexander's eyes to suspiciously flick over toward where they hid.

"I think, however, I know where he could be."

"I, ah, I best get back to the party," Cecily said, standing, as she patted her hair and dress back into place.

"Very well," Alexander said dismissively. "Enjoy."

As she flounced out of the room, he turned and looked in the direction where Elijah and Joanna were crouched. Elijah took Joanna's hand and led her out to face him.

"That was quite the little scheme."

Elijah shrugged. "You each wanted a liaison," he said, "so we provided you with the opportunity."

He led Joanna to the sofa where Cecily had been waiting just a few minutes before, and they sat down and faced Alexander.

"Alex, won't you sit down?" Elijah said, waving a hand to one of the chairs across from them.

"I'd rather not."

"Oh, come off it. You deserved far worse than that, and you know it. There is something that you have to say to us, is there not? An apology, perhaps?"

Alexander lifted his chin. "I do not."

"I just don't understand," Joanna said, shaking her head. "Why did you do it?"

Alexander looked back and forth from one of them to the other. "I was looking out for my brother," he said with a shrug.

"What do you mean?" Elijah said darkly.

"She's a seamstress," he said, lifting his hand toward Joanna. "She would make a fine mistress, yes, but do you truly want to *marry* a seamstress?"

"Yes," Elijah said, standing now. "I do truly want to marry a seamstress. None of your scheming or ill will is going to keep that from happening, and unless you would now like to apologize to Joanna, I believe this conversation is finished."

"Not quite yet."

They looked to the doorway to find their father and Lord Baxter standing within it.

"I was looking for you, Elijah," his father said in his deep voice. "I was told you came this way, and, as it happens, I am rather glad that I heard this conversation."

"Then you know that I wish to marry Joanna," Elijah stated, and Joanna's heart began to trip at the possibilities of his father's reaction.

It turned out, she didn't have to worry.

"Yes, and I think she is a fine choice," he said with a small smile for Joanna, who raised her brows, awestruck that he might actually agree.

He widened his hands out in front of him.

"If your sister can marry a footman, Elijah, then you can marry a seamstress. What this Christmas has taught me is that I would rather have you here with the family and happy, than for you to not be part of our lives any longer. And, in fact, there is something I would like to speak to you about. You as well, Alex."

They both looked at him with attention, and Joanna stepped forward and placed her hand on Elijah's back, ready to support him in whatever his father had to share.

"As you know, our family owns a few small estates. There is one in particular that I have intended for one of you to look after. Until this point, I wasn't sure which of you could take on the responsibility of doing so. I had always thought it would be Alex, but I decided to wait until you returned from war, Eli, to give you a fair chance at it."

He paused for a moment, clearing his throat. "And, I think... it's a good thing I waited. I can hardly believe it, but you would be the best fit, Elijah. Yes, I know you can sell your commission and could likely live off of that for a time, but you are a man who requires purpose to infuse your energy into or else you use that energy for other means. I believe that you and your bride can make a good life for yourselves. It is not overly far away, and the people will like you — for they will like her." He laughed. "So... what do you say?"

Elijah turned to look at Joanna, his eyes wide and rather incredulous.

"I... I don't know *what* to say," he said, and she knew without his words that he was asking what she thought. She smiled and gave a nod. It sounded like more than she could ever have asked for.

"We would be very appreciative, Father," Elijah said. "Thank you."

He reached out his hand and his father grasped it in a firm handshake. There was a raucous cry from the ballroom beyond and his father patted Elijah on the shoulder with something akin to affection.

"Well, what do you say we go back and join the rest of them? Sounds as though we are missing out on quite the Twelfth Night."

"Let's go then," Elijah said, and the lot of them filed out — even Alexander, who followed sullenly silent behind, his hands in his pockets.

"You've plenty of options, Alex," their father said, obviously also noting his son's dismay. "Just prove yourself."

Before they heard Alexander's response, Elijah took Joanna's hand and pulled her from the room. They stopped in the corridor before continuing onto the ballroom.

"The truth is, I don't care what Alex decides to do with his life," he murmured as he took her hands and held them close. "I think he knew about my father's choice and tried to ruin everything for us. All I care now is about the future — which is you and me, together. There's no mistletoe above us anymore, but..."—

"I don't need mistletoe," she said with a laugh. "I can just imagine it."

"I see a lot of imagining in our future," he growled.

"There better be," she returned, and when her lips met his, it was the best Christmas gift she could ever ask for.

EPILOGUE

"I'm home!"

Elijah pushed open the door of their manor. They still had much work to do, but this had become home in every sense of the word. It wasn't overly large, but it was quiet. It was peaceful. It was theirs.

"There you are," Joanna said, greeting him at the front entrance. He shut the door quickly so that the cold air wouldn't chill the room. "I was getting worried about you."

"I was trying to find just the right one," he said. "It's outside the window."

He proudly pulled back the curtain, and Joanna peered out at the fallen tree that was now resting outside, perfect for their very first Yule Log.

"It's wonderful," she said, walking over to him and leaning up for a kiss. "Thank you. You must be tired."

"I am," he said, following her in, appreciating the warm glow of the fire. "But likely not nearly as tired as you."

"Now *that* is the truth," she said as he removed his greatcoat and then lifted the bundle from her arms, cradling their son in his hands as he sat down on the sofa before the fire.

"He's beautiful."

Joanna chuckled. "You say that every time you see him."

"And yet it still holds true. John Edward. He looks just like his mother."

She leaned behind him, wrapping her arms around his neck and kissing his temple.

"Oh, I think he has much of his father in him, too."

"Hopefully not my mind," he said ruefully, and Joanna swatted him lightly.

"Your mind is beautiful and just as worthy," she said. "You've lost a few memories, yes, but that is simply part of who you are and what has happened to you. Besides, you are remembering more and more all of the time."

"This is true," he mused. "Perhaps it is because the memories I make now are worth keeping."

"Perhaps they are," she said with a smile. "A letter came for you while you were out."

"Oh?" he said, not particularly caring about it. "From whom?"

"From a Juanita Suarez."

He stilled. "Juanita… it couldn't be—"

But it had to be.

"Have you opened it?"

"No, of course not," Joanna said, rounding the chesterfield and sitting next to him.

"Go ahead," he said, nodding to her, not willing to relinquish the baby currently in his arms.

She broke the seal of the letter and unfolded it before she began to read.

"Elijah, I hope you are well and you were able to find your way home. You were very kind to me when I was in such distress. You were so concerned for my story and the plight of my lost love, that I felt compelled to write to you and tell you the end of it.

Last year, on Christmas morning, I was alone, hardly even

aware of what day it was, let alone in a mind to celebrate. You can imagine my utter astonishment when I saw someone limping down the walkway to my home." Joanna stopped and looked up. "It is just like your story."

"It is eerily similar," he noted, as she continued.

"It was Eduardo. I was wild with shock, sure that I was just seeing things, that it could not actually be him. I ran out to him, caught him, helped him back into the house. I was the only one home, my father out. Oh, Elijah, how wonderful it was to see him again. He was the same man as he had been before, yet so different in the same breath. He had been injured, a bullet having gone through his shoulder and another through his leg, but he was home. He was otherwise healthy. And he still loved me. We were married three months later. I only hope that you have found the same happiness as I have. Farewell, Elijah."

There were tears in Joanna's eyes as she finished the letter.

"The true ending is much better than yours."

"On that, you are correct," he said with a laugh. "We shall have to update everyone on what has occurred."

"They won't be pleased you lied."

He shrugged. "It returned your watch to you, did it not?"

"It did," Joanna said with a small smile, just as the door opened.

"Elijah, you're back!" Caroline explained. "Thatcher was just about to come look for you. He had hoped to finish early enough to join you."

"There is much to be done, Caro," Elijah said to his sister. "Come, have a seat."

"I don't suppose you will give up that baby to me to hold, will you?"

"Not yet," he said, laughing lowly so as not to wake his son. "Besides, you have one of your own."

Their arrangement had worked out perfectly thus far.

Elijah had required a steward to help him with his estate. Thatcher had been caught in a strange situation of becoming family without the education to take on a profession that would be seen as respectable for a man with a noble wife.

Working with Elijah had been the solution for all of them, and Joanna had appreciated having Caroline nearby so they could raise their children together..

"Do you mind not going home this year for the entire Christmastide party?" Elijah asked Caroline just as Thatcher joined them.

"Not at all," Caroline said, shaking her head. "Seeing the family for Christmas and Twelfth Night will be just perfect, don't you think, Jo?"

"I absolutely do," Joanna agreed with a smile. "This year I have no reason to avoid Briercrest."

She laughed as she looked over at Elijah with a spark in her eyes, and he winked back at her.

"Now you can't get rid of me."

"Behave yourself, and I will never see reason to."

As Elijah held the baby tightly in his arms, he had to blink back the tears that threatened — tears that all he had never thought possible had come to be. A family of his own, a wife who loved him, and a home to fill with memories for the rest of his life.

And just in case he forgot some of them... Joanna was there to remind him.

THE END

* * *

Dear reader,

I hope you enjoyed reading Joanna and Elijah's story! Every year I look forward to writing (and reading) Christmas stories. If you enjoyed this one, I have a few more to share. Most are standalone novels, but they all contain your favorite Christmas traditions and a happily ever after.

I've included the first chapter of Her Christmas Wish for you in the upcoming pages, and at the end of the book there is a list of all my other Christmas stories.

If you haven't yet signed up for my newsletter, I would love to have you join! You will receive a free book, as well as links to giveaways, sales, new releases, and stories about my coffee addiction, my struggle to keep my plants alive, and how much trouble one loveable wolf-lookalike dog can get into.

www.elliestclair.com/ellies-newsletter

Or you can join my Facebook group, Ellie St. Clair's Ever Afters, and stay in touch daily.

If you are reading this during the holiday season, I hope you have a very Merry Christmas!
With love,
Ellie

***

Her Christmas Wish

LORD CHARLES BLYTHE **impulsively chooses the first woman he sees as a fake bride. What happens when he discovers she's a governess?**

Charles must produce an heir to prevent his loathsome cousin or the man's obnoxious son from inheriting. Since the death of his wife, he has had no desire to wed any of the young, empty-headed women that society thrusts at him. Emily Nicholls seems perfect.

Except the one thing Charles needs, Emily cannot provide. The same Christmas wish has haunted her for years — to have a family of her own – but after six years of marriage resulted in no children, the widowed Emily began to care for others instead, although it does not quite fill the hole in her heart.

When Charles convinces Emily to join his family for Christmas, they find themselves tempted. They will have to decide which Christmas wish should come true – love, or duty?

* * *

AN EXCERPT FROM HER CHRISTMAS WISH

Lord and Lady Coningsby had outdone themselves once again.

Charles stood at the top of the stairs as he looked at the ballroom before him. He was announced — alone — though no one paid much attention. There were glances from some of the eligible young women and their mothers, of course, but most who would be invited tonight had already done their utmost to capture his attention.

While Charles appreciated the effort, he simply wasn't interested. Soon enough, he would find someone suitable. He just hadn't the energy at the moment.

"Doverton!" Lord Coningsby exclaimed as Charles reached the bottom of the stairs. "It's good to see you again, old chap. It has been a minute, has it not?"

Charles smiled at the man who stood next to the stairwell with his wife on his arm. The two of them had found contentment with one another, which Charles looked upon with both pleasure for his friend and his own bit of envy. If only he and Miriam had found the same with one another… but that no longer mattered, so why dwell on the past?

"I have been in London for a few months now and only returned a week ago," Charles said, coming back to the moment and assuming his practiced smile for occasions such as this. "I would have called upon you earlier, but I knew you would be deep in preparations for this evening."

Coningsby laughed heartily. "Alexandra here was, of course, but I would have welcomed the distraction. You would think this would become easier year after year, but alas, it remains as much work as ever. Now, there are plenty here who are looking forward to speaking with you."

"My family?" Charles asked with a raised eyebrow. "I see Anita over there, as well as Katrina."

"Of course," Coningsby said with the slightest of smirks, for he knew Charles' true feelings regarding his cousins, "but I was speaking of a few young ladies. You aren't getting any younger, you know, Doverton, and since Miriam has been gone some time now— ouch!"

Were they speaking of another subject, Charles would have enjoyed Lady Coningsby's unsubtle reproach to her husband's topic of conversation, but he would prefer that none of them continued to speak of this.

"I may not be getting any younger, but it seems the eligible women are," Charles said, filling the silence as he surveyed the room. "Why, many of the women looking my way are young enough to be my daughter."

"*That* is certainly no way to create a romantic sentiment," said Coningsby, chuckling. "But you do have your succession to think of."

Charles sighed.

"That, my friend, is my greatest concern."

Coningsby nodded in understanding before Charles took his leave to find himself a drink, hearing Lady Coningsby chastising her husband as he walked away. Coningsby had never had much ability to determine just when he should speak and of what, but Charles actually enjoyed that about the man. It was far better to know what to expect.

He had just taken his first sip of brandy, welcoming its warm sensation sliding down his throat, when he heard his name being called. Recognizing the voice, he prepared himself so that when he turned, his distaste would not be evident within his expression.

Apparently, he was not as successful as he would have thought.

"Coningsby serving cheap brandy?" his cousin Edward asked as he approached. Charles attempted to sink into the wall behind him, but that only served to back him into the stone, where a tall angel with pink wings awaited.

Despite Edward being the same age as him, the two of them had never gotten on well. Perhaps it was because Edward had coveted everything Charles had ever called his own — including Miriam.

Unfortunately, the title, the estate, and all that it entailed would fall to Edward were anything to ever happen to Charles, for he had no other siblings and Edward was the closest blood relative.

Charles hadn't been disappointed in having a daughter. In fact, he could still remember the euphoria, the love that he had never before felt tugging at his heart the moment he held the tiny baby in his arms.

But that was before. Before the miscarriages. Before Miriam's icy politeness grew into a hostility that barred him from entering her room. Before she had not only kept his own child from him but had turned her against him.

Before Charles had to come to terms with the fact that he would never have a son, and all would, one day, be lost.

There hadn't been anything to be done about it. And then Miriam had died, and Charles couldn't imagine himself going through all of that once more, though of all the responsibilities he held, perhaps seeing to his line was the greatest. He had never been able to let go of his father's teachings — of the importance of ensuring the male line survived.

He would find a wife. A young, fertile wife who would provide him with plenty of sons. He just had to be sure of one thing — after the pain of losing his daughter's affections, he would never fall in love again.

* * *

"I NEED MY DOLL, Holly, Mrs. Nicholls," Henrietta said in a quiet voice, her voluminous blue eyes pleading with Emily.

Emily sighed inwardly. She seemed to spend more time searching for Henrietta's well-loved wooden doll than she did looking after the children.

"And where is it, darling?" Emily asked with as much patience as she could muster as she crouched down in front of the girl. Henrietta bit her lip and hung her head so that she didn't have to meet Emily's eyes.

"Henrietta?"

"Just tell her, Hen," Michael offered from across the room, looking up from his book. They were sitting in the nursery, though the room was no longer fitting for young children. Emily had reformatted it into a library of sorts, and a secondary place where they could work on their lessons when the actual library was unavailable.

"I can only find it if you tell me where it is," Emily said after taking a deep breath. "You know how important it is to be honest with one another."

"The ballroom," Henrietta whispered, looking up at Emily with regret in her eyes. "Behind the last row of chairs in the corner beside the angel with the long pink wings."

"The ballroom? Good heavens, Henrietta, what is it doing in there?"

"I wanted to see the ballroom beautifully decorated before the party began, and I must have left my doll in the corner when the housekeeper caught me sneaking through."

"Henrietta, we shall have to get it tomorrow. You know the ballroom is currently filled with all of your parents' friends."

"Oh, please, Mrs. Nicholls, we *must* find it tonight! I cannot sleep without Holly, you know I simply cannot! And what if someone takes her? She could be gone by morning!"

Emily pushed a few stray strands of hair back from her forehead. She certainly had no wish to enter the ballroom, full of the viscount and viscountess' noble friends, but Henrietta had a point. If that doll was lost, there would be tears for many nights to come. Better to suffer through a moment of embarrassment to save both Henrietta and herself some pain later on.

"Very well," she said with a sigh. "Sit down, now. I'll be right back. Then it is straight to bed — no stalling, all right?"

"Oh, thank you, Mrs. Nicholls," Henrietta said, all smiles now. "I do love you, you know."

"And I, you. Now, I'll be right back."

Emily hurried down the long corridor, her hand on the balcony, before reaching the staircase to the ground floor. The symphony of music grew ever louder as she took one stair after another before she finally reached the landing. Here, maids and footmen scurried back and forth, refilling drinks, adding food to the sideboard, and fetching cloaks and hats.

Hopefully, she could find her way through the throng without being noticed. She supposed she looked enough like any other servant who was moving amongst the guests, though she was dressed slightly better than the maids who served food and drink.

She tiptoed to the door of the ballroom, although it was not as though she had to be quiet — somehow it made her feel less likely to be noticed. The pink angel was painted upon the wall in the farthest corner, of course. Emily decided she would keep to the outskirts of the ballroom so as not to be observed, particularly by Lord and Lady Coningsby.

Emily had to admit that she could see what had drawn Henrietta to the room. It was stunning as it was, but even more so with white lilies from the conservatory placed in lavish vases ornamenting the room, along with laurel, holly, ivy, and pine, already draped around the columns in preparation for the coming Christmas season.

If that wasn't enough, the people who filled it nearly overwhelmed her senses. Her ears rang and she was nearly dizzy from the scents and sights. Women were draped in extravagant gowns of every color, jewels dripping from their ears and down their necks. Their hair was curled and twisted into knots more elaborate than anything Emily had ever seen. Her entire family could probably live off the cost of one of those dresses for an entire year, she thought ruefully, but then shook her head.

Enough of that. She was lucky to be here and to work for such people.

Emily pushed her spectacles back up her nose as she returned her focus to finding Emily's doll instead of ogling the guests of her employer's ball.

The wooden doll. She would find it quickly, and then back upstairs she would go — to her rightful place.

* * *

"Hello, Edward," Charles greeted his cousin.

Unfortunately, Edward looked much like him, enough that the two of them had been mistaken for brothers many times before.

Fortunately, they were not.

"Charles," Edward said with a wide grin. "I'm happy to see you. Our visits are much too seldom."

Or too frequent.

"What keeps you busy these days, Edward?" Charles asked, bringing his drink to his lips.

"This and that. Keeping my wife happy. Raising my children. Doing what I can to prepare Thaddeus for his inheritance."

"Oh? Did you come into money recently?" Charles asked dryly, to which Edward laughed.

"I mean the title, Charles! You've but a daughter, and it looks to me like there will not be another Lady Doverton judging from the interest — or lack of — you have shown any lady. Just as well. I will look after the title someday, Charles, as will Thaddeus. Ah, don't look so glum about it. We'll take good care of things for you. In fact, Leticia has already begun to plan her renovations to Ravenport — as countess or dowager."

There had already been more than enough renovations to Ravenport for his liking thanks to his wife. He wasn't going to settle for any more — particularly from Leticia. He had seen Edward's home, and he had no desire for his manor to follow suit.

"I did not realize my demise was imminent."

"No, no, Charles, of course not," chuckled Edward. "However, Thaddeus and I have had many discussions about the manor. While you do your best, I'm sure, you are slightly too... generous. Your servants seem as well off as you, and sometimes I question whether your tenants are working for you, or if you are working for your tenants!"

Charles' teeth ground together of their own accord at the thought of his lands and his people in the hands of Edward or Thaddeus. Edward's son was a rake of the worst sort — Charles had heard rumors that the man not only found himself in the beds of quite a number of women, but some were less willing than others. Good Lord, what would happen to his lands in the hands of either of the two of these men? It had taken long enough for Charles to correct many of his own father's mistakes. It pained him to think of all he had done erased once more.

"Thinking of the good times to come, Charles?" Edward drawled out, a gleam in his eye.

Charles straightened and looked Edward right in the eye.

"Actually, as it happens, I am to be married very soon."

He wasn't sure where those words had come from. He most definitely was *not* planning on marrying soon. Or at all. But he had no desire to allow Edward to continue to believe he would be taking his place. It was time to put to an end any mention of these plans.

"You are not getting married," Edward said with a smirk. "I am sure it would be on the tongues of all the London gossips."

"We have kept things rather quiet," Charles said as confidently as he could, creating his story as he spoke. "It is a second marriage for both of us, you see."

"Ah," Edward said with a gleam in his eye, clearly still not believing Charles. "And just who is the lucky lady? I am surprised that she is not here with you."

"But of course she is," Charles said smoothly. "She will return soon, I am sure."

"Oh, come, Charles, you are making this all up," Edward said with a laugh. "You have never been much of a liar. Just tell the truth of it, man, and be done with it. Is it really such a horrible thought that I might inherit your land?"

It really was.

"My soon-to-be-bride is here. Of course she is," Charles said, turning his neck, catching sight of a blond head coming straight toward him. A quick glance told him she didn't seem to be anyone he knew. "Here she is now."

He reached out and took the lady's hand just as she was about to pass by him, hoping that whoever she was, she would go along with his ploy for just a few minutes. Then he would figure something else out later on, but for now, he had to preserve his honor in front of his cousin.

The cousin whose face was currently frozen in shock.

Charles hastily turned around. Once he caught sight of the woman, he couldn't turn away.

The first thing to capture Charles' attention was her dress. It was... serviceable, if he was being generous with his description. A navy, boxy creation, it was difficult to determine her shape beneath it. Next came her hair. A sandy blond, it was pulled tightly back away from her head, and on her nose perched a pair of spectacles. Through them, her wide brown eyes stared at him incredulously, her fingers nervously touching her throat.

Well, like it or not, this was the woman he had chosen to be his wife.

For the next few minutes, at least.

* * *

Keep reading Her Christmas Wish!

ALSO BY ELLIE ST. CLAIR

Christmas Books
A Match Made at Christmas
A Match Made in Winter

Christmastide with His Countess
Her Christmas Wish
Merry Misrule
Duke of Christmas
Duncan's Christmas

Reckless Rogues
The Earls's Secret
The Viscount's Code
The Scholar's Key
Prequel, The Duke's Treasure, available in:
I Like Big Dukes and I Cannot Lie

The Remingtons of the Regency
The Mystery of the Debonair Duke
The Secret of the Dashing Detective
The Clue of the Brilliant Bastard
The Quest of the Reclusive Rogue

The Unconventional Ladies
Lady of Mystery
Lady of Fortune

Lady of Providence

Lady of Charade

The Unconventional Ladies Box Set

To the Time of the Highlanders

A Time to Wed

A Time to Love

A Time to Dream

Thieves of Desire

The Art of Stealing a Duke's Heart

A Jewel for the Taking

A Prize Worth Fighting For

Gambling for the Lost Lord's Love

Romance of a Robbery

Thieves of Desire Box Set

The Bluestocking Scandals

[Designs on a Duke](#)

[Inventing the Viscount](#)

[Discovering the Baron](#)

[The Valet Experiment](#)

[Writing the Rake](#)

[Risking the Detective](#)

[A Noble Excavation](#)

[A Gentleman of Mystery](#)

The Bluestocking Scandals Box Set: Books 1-4

The Bluestocking Scandals Box Set: Books 5-8

Blooming Brides
A Duke for Daisy
A Marquess for Marigold
An Earl for Iris
A Viscount for Violet

The Blooming Brides Box Set: Books 1-4

Happily Ever After
The Duke She Wished For
Someday Her Duke Will Come
Once Upon a Duke's Dream
He's a Duke, But I Love Him
Loved by the Viscount
Because the Earl Loved Me

Happily Ever After Box Set Books 1-3
Happily Ever After Box Set Books 4-6

The Victorian Highlanders
Duncan's Christmas - (prequel)
Callum's Vow
Finlay's Duty
Adam's Call
Roderick's Purpose
Peggy's Love

The Victorian Highlanders Box Set Books 1-5

Searching Hearts
Duke of Christmas (prequel)

Quest of Honor

Clue of Affection

Hearts of Trust

Hope of Romance

Promise of Redemption

Searching Hearts Box Set (Books 1-5)

Standalones

Always Your Love

The Stormswept Stowaway

A Touch of Temptation

For a full list of all of Ellie's books, please see www.elliestclair.com/books.

ABOUT THE AUTHOR

Ellie has always loved reading, writing, and history. For many years she has written short stories, non-fiction, and has worked on her true love and passion -- romance novels.

In every era there is the chance for romance, and Ellie enjoys exploring many different time periods, cultures, and geographic locations. No matter when or where, love can always prevail. She has a particular soft spot for the bad boys of history, and loves a strong heroine in her stories.

Ellie and her husband love nothing more than spending time at home with their children and Husky cross. Ellie can typically be found at the lake in the summer, pushing the stroller all year round, and, of course, with her computer in her lap or a book in hand.

She also loves corresponding with readers, so be sure to contact her!

www.elliestclair.com
ellie@elliestclair.com

Printed in Great Britain
by Amazon